THE QUEEN'S NOSE:
HARMONY'S RETURN

When she thought her chest was going to burst Harmony reached a small fountain. A sheet of water cascaded down and she sat beside it, cupping her hands in the water and splashing it on her face.

'Who is going to help us now?' she asked aloud.

'Who indeed?' someone replied.

Harmony looked up and there, behind the falling water, was her Uncle Ginger's face. Harmony put her hand through the sheet of water and the face disappeared. When she withdrew her hand the face reappeared.

'How did you know I was here?' she asked.

'I always know when people I care about are miserable,' Ginger said, smiling.

The Queen's Nose:
Harmony's Return

Novelization by Steve Attridge
Adapted from the screenplay by Steve Attridge
Based on the characters created by Dick King-Smith
in the original novel *The Queen's Nose*

PUFFIN BOOKS

PUFFIN BOOKS

Published by the Penguin Group
Penguin Books Ltd, 27 Wrights Lane, London W8 5TZ, England
Penguin Books USA Inc., 375 Hudson Street, New York, New York 10014, USA
Penguin Books Australia Ltd, Ringwood, Victoria, Australia
Penguin Books Canada Ltd, 10 Alcorn Avenue, Toronto, Ontario, Canada M4V 3B2
Penguin Books (NZ) Ltd, 182–190 Wairau Road, Auckland 10, New Zealand

Penguin Books Ltd, Registered Offices: Harmondsworth, Middlesex, England

Published in Puffin Books 1996

1 3 5 7 9 10 8 6 4 2

Puffin Film and TV Tie-in edition first published 1996

Text copyright © Steve Attridge, 1996
All rights reserved

The Queen's Nose
First published by Victor Gollancz 1983
Published in Puffin Books 1985
Copyright © Dick King-Smith, 1983

The moral right of the author has been asserted

Set in Monotype Bembo
Typeset by Rowland Phototypesetting Ltd,
Bury St Edmunds, Suffolk
Printed in England by Clays Ltd, St Ives plc

It was the worst day of her life and someone was going to pay for it. The hardest thing had been saying goodbye to the animals. One of Harmony's friends had agreed to look after Anita the rabbit and Lucky the dog, but it didn't make it any easier. Harmony Parker was leaving a lot of things behind that day, but leaving the animals was definitely the worst.

'I wish I could stay with you,' she said, giving Anita a last stroke of her long, silky ears and Lucky a pat on the head.

She also wished she still had the Queen's Nose. 'Our family could do with a bit of wishing magic right now,' Harmony said to herself as she watched the pets being taken into her friend's parents' car. She wondered what had happened to the magic coin that her Uncle Ginger had given her. Her thoughts were interrupted by the tooting of a car horn. She turned to see a removal truck pulling away from her house and a taxi containing her family waiting for her. Of course, it wasn't her house any more. She would have to get used to that. She had been born there. She knew every crack in the walls, every creak of the stairs, every hole left by a drawing-pin in her bedroom wall from numerous pictures that charted her life from

Noddy to Guns n' Roses. And now she was leaving them all.

And this made her fed up. Very fed up indeed. And Harmony fully intended to make someone pay for just how fed up she was. Someone's nerves would be ragged by the time they all got out of the taxi, and they would not be hers. She scowled as she got in the back of the taxi, her mother on her right and Melody, her sister, on the other side. Like sitting between two gargoyles, Harmony thought. Mr Parker sat in front with the driver. She waited for someone to speak. It wouldn't matter what they said, because anything would do as a trigger for her anger.

'I'm truly sorry about having to leave your pets,' Mrs Parker said.

This was her chance. 'It's not fair,' Harmony said, spitting out the words.

'No, but we have to leave, darling. We have no choice since your father's little problem at work,' Mrs Parker replied.

'Little problem? Huh! I thought he got sacked. I thought there was a financial scandal. Everyone seems to think Dad's a master criminal. Sounds like a *big* problem to me.'

Harmony could see her father's ears turning pink with embarrassment. The driver gave him a sidelong glance.

'No need to tell the whole world, Harmony,' Mr Parker muttered.

'Hard times, eh, guv'nor?' the driver asked.

'Hard times! More like complete disaster, end of the world time' – Harmony was getting into her stride now – 'and Dad, you said the world was full of conmen and pirates and people who cheat you in restaurants and in taxis and you'd never trust anyone again and . . .'

'Yes, yes, I was upset at the time,' Mr Parker said, his ears going from pink to bright red.

Harmony wondered what colour they would go next if she carried on. She decided to put the ears to the test. 'More like completely off your chump,' she said, then nodded at Melody, 'and old sissie here's got the hump because we've got to move.'

'You've got the hump, more like. That's probably why your breath smells like a camel's,' Melody muttered miserably.

'I think you mean a dromedary, ignoramus Melodius,' Harmony said, relishing the scoring of another point over her sister.

Mrs Parker had had enough. 'Just stop all this bickering! We should all thank our lucky stars that my mother's back from Paris and that she's kindly invited us to stay until we get on our feet again.'

Grandma was waiting outside the mansion block and looked even worse than Harmony remembered. She had fluffy pink hair, was wearing a feather boa and old holey trainers. She had fiercely glittering eyes and a mouth that hated full stops. The granny from hell. The nutter from

North Acton. As a very little girl Harmony had imagined that Grandma washed her hair in bat droppings and pulled the wings off ladybirds as a hobby. Harmony decided that she definitely would not be seen in public with her. The feeling was mutual. Gran had not taken kindly to her ever since the day, as a little girl, Harmony had put itching powder in her bloomers and drawing-pins in her porridge. Or was it the other way round? Harmony couldn't quite remember.

Things started badly. Grandma called Harmony 'Herman' and behaved as if Mr Parker didn't exist as she took them upstairs, commiserating with Mrs Parker and embarrassing everybody.

'My poor darling, the shame, the humiliation. If only you hadn't married beneath you. My heart bleeds for you. A mother always suffers with her child. It's almost religious.' And so on. And on and on and on.

When they got inside the flat everyone was shocked except Grandma. She had been back from Paris for six months but, typically, had only let them know a few weeks ago. She had led them to believe that the flat was luxuriously decorated and they could feel at home as long as they wished in this second-to-none palace. The fact was that she had done nothing in six months. Crates were still packed, carpets rolled up, boxes unopened. Walls had had a stroke of paint here and there in different colours until Grandma had obviously, rapidly, got bored. The kitchen had no cooker or fridge. The boiler was not working so there was no hot water in the bathroom. The whole place was a dusty, uncomfortable mess.

Grandma led them to a small bedroom, full of grubby crates.

'I'm sure there was a bed in here somewhere,' Grandma said, lifting dust-sheets. 'Ah. Here.' She lifted a sheet and barely visible in a dust cloud were bunk-beds. 'Here you are, Herman. You'll find some blankets around somewhere, or perhaps you prefer to wrap yourself in newspaper, given that you dress like an old tramp.'

'Not like you, eh, Gran? I hope your dress designer is still in prison.'

The worst thing was that Melody had to share the room. Melody was appalled. Having to breathe the same air, having to listen to Harmony burp and snort and giggle and snore like a demented gorilla in her sleep. It really would drive her mad. Harmony commented that it would be a very short drive.

The adults left the girls arguing and Grandma led Mrs Parker to another room. Mr Parker followed, feeling more miserable with each moment.

'And you'll be sleeping in here, dear,' Gran said, indicating the uninviting little room which contained a single bed and nothing else.

'But, Mother, there's only a single bed. What about Arthur?'

Grandma ignored the question and left.

'Pinch me, just to make sure I exist,' Mr Parker said.

'Oh, she'll come round. She's just . . .'

'Escaped from a dragon farm? Twenty teeth short of a full set? Oh, I'm sorry, I didn't see you there, I . . .' Mr Parker trailed off as Grandma magically appeared again with a cup of tea for Mrs Parker. It was as if she hadn't heard Mr Parker's insults.

Grandma didn't cook. It was a matter of principle with her. She prided herself on not having prepared a meal for twenty-three years. So Mrs Parker warmed up a few tins of soup on a tiny camping-stove and Grandma found some plastic spoons and a wooden crate to use as a table, and laid places for everyone except Mr Parker.

'You can't keep behaving as if Arthur doesn't exist,' Mrs Parker said.

'As if who doesn't exist, dear?' Grandma replied sweetly.

Just as Mr Parker was thinking that things couldn't get any worse, they did. A Fraud Squad officer arrived at the flat to question him again. He had answered the same questions so many times he felt like screaming. Yes, he kept the information about customers on a computer disk which he locked in the company safe every night. He had certainly not sold this information to other finance companies. No, he knew nothing about the phoney share certificates and no, it was definitely not his signature on them.

Harmony watched from the kitchen doorway and could

see that the officer didn't believe a word her father said. She hated what she saw. It was one thing for her to tell Mr Parker he was a criminal and to make fun of him in public. She had a right to do it. She was his daughter and that's what children did. This man, who looked like a woodpecker, his beaky face stabbing the air as he asked questions, was a complete stranger.

The officer was holding a piece of paper in front of Mr Parker and asking him for the third time, 'Is this your signature or not?'

'You people keep saying it is,' Mr Parker said, his temper rising.

'And what do you say, sir?' the officer sneered.

'I say I am sick and tired of these questions. I say I am innocent. I say someone else committed these crimes. I say I am being framed!'

Harmony could feel her father's frustration and anger. He also looked desperate and she had never seen that in his face before. It chilled her and, to her surprise, her vision misted as her eyes filled with tears. Suddenly she wanted to be outside, running, with the sounds of traffic roaring in her ears. She dashed out of the flat, clattered down the stairs, out of the block and along the road. She ran until her chest hurt, expertly dodging between people, her face grimy and tear-stained. She ran until she came to a park and raced across the grass, the noises of the city receding behind her.

When she thought her chest was going to burst

Harmony reached a small fountain. A sheet of water cascaded down and she sat beside it, cupping her hands in the water and splashing it on her face.

'Who is going to help us now?' she asked aloud.

'Who indeed?' someone replied.

Harmony looked up and there, behind the falling water, was her Uncle Ginger's face. Harmony put her hand through the sheet of water and the face disappeared. When she withdrew her hand the face reappeared.

'How did you know I was here?' she asked.

'I always know when people I care about are miserable,' Ginger said, smiling.

Mr Parker's brother, Ginger, had begun life as a strange little boy and had continued to get stranger, as if he didn't know when to stop. So, despite the initial shock, Harmony wasn't completely surprised to see his face in such an unusual place. It was Ginger who first gave the Queen's Nose to Harmony – the fifty-pence piece which enabled her wishes to come true, though not always as she had hoped.

She told him of the Fraud Squad pestering her father, of how awful it was at Grandma's flat, of how crabby and horrible she was being to Harmony and her dad.

'I didn't know things were that bad,' Ginger said, after he had listened to Harmony's tale of woe. 'We must help you all. Especially your father.'

'How?'

'With a bit of ingenuity, a bit of thought, a bit of love,

and a sprinkling of magic. Say the words, Harmony.'

'Which words?'

Ginger smiled, and she understood.

'The Queen's Nose,' she said.

'Open sesame,' Ginger said.

His hand reached out through the water, the fist closed tightly. This was a real hand, not a reflection or make-believe. Harmony noticed the drops of water glistening on the nut-brown skin, the tiny hairs, the whiteness of the knuckles. The hand opened and there was the coin, wrapped in a piece of paper. She took off the paper and looked at it. It seemed to be an ordinary coin, but she knew better. For an instant, the tip of the Queen's Nose glinted. It may have been sunlight playing off the water, but Harmony knew it was something that came from the coin itself. The coin seemed to tingle in her hand. Perhaps it recognizes me? she thought.

'You going to spend all night talking to it?' She looked up. Uncle Ginger had gone, but behind her were six boys, all about fifteen years old, all staring down at her. Rough old lot, she thought. Ugly too, but better not tell them that.

'Or you going to give it to us?' said a boy with a shaven head.

'Give what?' Harmony asked.

'The coin. Only we're collecting for charity,' Baldy said.

'The needy orphans of Choke Hill,' another boy said.

'Yeah, we need a bag of chips,' Baldy said.

'Don't you mean the nerds of Choke Hill who need brain transplants?' Harmony said. She knew it was stupid but she couldn't help herself.

'Just give it here,' Baldy snarled, grabbing her hand and bending her closed fingers back until her fist opened. Two of the boys seized Harmony and held her arms behind her back. Baldy held the coin. The two boys let Harmony go.

'Thanks. We'll have the chips, you look for the fish,' Baldy said, and shoved Harmony so hard that she fell backwards into the fountain.

Near by, in the shadows beneath a tree, stood another boy. The gang approached him and he held out his hand. Baldy gave him the coin. The hand closed over the coin as if trying to stifle it. On its middle finger a ring glinted.

CHAPTER 2

If Harmony had expected any sympathy from her family, which she didn't, she would have been disappointed. As she trailed miserably through the flat, dripping mud and grass, Grandma called her a revolting little creature, so Harmony accidentally-on-purpose knocked a tin of paint over Gran's feet as she passed. Melody laughed and hoped that Harmony would be very happy in her new pond home. Sitting on her bed, she noticed a little scuffling thing in the corner of the room. She went over and there was a mouse, standing up on its hind legs, completely unafraid and staring at her with its glittering eyes.

'Hello,' Harmony said, and picked up the mouse. He had a big sniff of her hand and didn't seem to mind the smell at all. 'I shall call you Monty.'

After she had made a small house for Monty from an old bird cage she found in the hall, she ran upstairs, through the fire-escape door and on to the roof. She approached the edge and looked down. The cars were like matchbox toys, people like busy beetles, scuttling across roads, crossing and re-crossing, all bustling about with some purpose or other. In the dark the whole city was like an animated map. Heights didn't bother Harmony. In fact, standing way above everything made her feel quite peaceful. Losing the coin, being bullied by those cretins in the park, which had been frightening, seemed a long time ago. It wasn't that being on the roof solved anything, it just made it seem a long way off, like looking at things through the wrong end of a telescope. And she had found a splendid new friend called Monty.

Harmony heard a sigh and looked around. She had thought she was alone. To her surprise, she recognized Mr Parker on the other side of the roof, looking up at the sky.

'Wishing you could fly away?' Harmony asked.

Mr Parker was startled, then smiled. 'Harmony! Yes, I wouldn't mind flying away sometimes. Just to not be me for a while.'

This was unlike her dad. He was always so very much . . . her dad. Mr Parker. Arthur. Father.

'Let's be something else, then. Let's be wolves,' Harmony said. 'We can bay at the moon. Like this.' Harmony held back her head and gave a magnificent howl, starting low and eerie, then opening her throat and really letting rip. Mr Parker watched for a moment, embarrassed, then thought, why not? He leaned his head back and gave a little whimpery growl, then a louder, throatier one, then a full-blooded wolf's howl.

Way below in the streets passers-by and cyclists stopped suddenly and looked up. A few were sure they could hear animals howling. Wolves, one man thought. Wolves in London? A woman looked up and on the top of the mansion block she could make out the shape of two wolves. Yes, there were two large wolves right up there on the roof, silhouetted against the moonlit sky, the outline of their long noses and sharp ears clearly visible. She shivered. She must be slightly feverish, imagining things. Best not to tell anyone. They wouldn't believe her anyway.

In the flat the noise above was truly eerie. Melody sat bolt upright in bed, banging her head on the top bunk. Mrs Parker, in the hall painting over some GRANNY GO BACK TO FRANCE graffiti by Harmony, stopped, her blood chilling at the sound above. Wolves? On the roof? Surely not. Sitting up in bed, reading a horror book, and scoffing chocolates, Grandma heard the howling and immediately reached under the bed for a very large blunderbuss left to her by her father.

Minutes later there was chaos on the roof. Mr Parker and Harmony were in the middle of a full-blown howl when Grandma pushed through the fire-escape door, followed by a distraught Mrs Parker holding a mop.

'Intruders! I'll show you. Think you can scare a poor defenceless old lady, do you?' Grandma yelled.

'Mother! Put down that gun! It's Arthur. Can't you see him?'

'Who?' Grandma said, for whom Mr Parker still did not exist. 'It's a burglar, I tell you.'

'Put down that gun!' Mrs Parker shrieked.

'It's just to scare them. It's not even loaded. See?'

Grandma squeezed the trigger and there was an almighty roar that stopped the traffic below. Mrs Parker fainted. Mr Parker ran to her. Grandma looked in stunned and admiring silence at the smoking gun.

And Harmony? She began to think that something was working against her and her family. It was time for a visit to Ginger. This time, she had to see him in person.

Ginger had opened a shop called Ginger's Genie. Harmony went there a great deal and loved it, but if anyone asked her what it sold, she had to think hard. It seemed to change each time she visited and although she had a good memory, she could never quite retain a picture of the shop interior in her mind. It was as if the shop was a chameleon, forever changing its appearance. A bit like Ginger himself.

Harmony entered the shop and was greeted by a tinkling of chimes and a smell of incense. It was dimly lit and like an Aladdin's cave of curiosities: boxes of magic tricks, animals carved in wood, oriental rugs with great swirls of colour and pattern, hookah pipes, jewellery, spices and paintings. Harmony suddenly realized that she had never seen a customer in there. Perhaps Uncle Ginger wanted a shop but not customers. He was like that.

'Uncle Ginger?'

No reply.

Harmony walked in further. In one corner a painting seemed to come to life and animals ran across it and disappeared. To her right an old-fashioned, mechanical toy merry-go-round started, but when she turned to look at it, it stopped. The head of a Balinese shadow-puppet nodded briefly. A suspended crocodile-puppet opened its jaws, then snapped them shut. Had it been anywhere else Harmony would have turned and run by now, but this all belonged to Uncle Ginger, so it had to be all right. Didn't it?

'Uncle Ginger?'

She brushed aside long flimsy drapes that hung like spidery nets from the ceiling, layer after layer, and there he was. Uncle Ginger sat cross-legged, his eyes closed, on a carpet that hovered two metres above the ground, as if held up by invisible hands or by a current of powerful air. Suddenly he opened his eyes and smiled. The carpet floated down to earth.

'How did you do that?' Harmony asked.

'With a great deal of effort,' Ginger said. He frowned and a web of tight little lines appeared around his eyes. 'I'm sorry about the coin.'

He knows already, Harmony thought. But that wasn't really a surprise. Ginger tended to know most things that happened. Sometimes he even had an idea about them before they happened.

'So what can I do? How can I get it back?' Harmony asked.

'Look,' Ginger said, picking up a large crystal from a table. Harmony looked at it and could see fragments of herself in the jagged surfaces. Here her nose, there an eye, there a flash of red hair. It looked like a modern painting, everything broken up into bits.

'Bits of me,' Harmony said.

'Look closer,' Ginger said, and shook the crystal.

Harmony looked again. Now she saw leaves and shadows dancing, then a clenched fist pushing through the leaves. On the middle finger a ring with a skull and cross-bones on it. The hand opened for a moment and the Queen's Nose flashed a sliver of light, then the hand closed again. Far off, Harmony thought she heard a bell ring. The picture faded and there was Uncle Ginger, smiling.

'Clues. Pictures to keep in your mind. Along with the riddle, of course.'

'What riddle?' Harmony asked.

'The one in your pocket.'

Sure enough, there was a piece of paper in her pocket. She read it:

> *One letter away from snub will give you a clue,*
> *knowing there are ten will help you too,*
> *they are yours, but then again, not —*
> *beware what you want — things may get too hot!*

'What does it mean, Uncle Ginger?'

But Ginger was off on his carpet again, floating, his eyes closed, in some private, blissful world all of his own.

Knowing Uncle Ginger, he could be like that for hours, so Harmony left. She was going to have to try and work out how to get the coin back for herself. And there was something else preying on her mind like a wasp that wouldn't leave her alone. Tomorrow she started at her new school.

Choke Hill High School had been a prison many years ago, and some children maintained that nothing had changed. A sprawling, dirty, spooky-looking building that immediately made visitors want to turn around and walk away. As Harmony entered the playground she attracted the attention of the head-teacher, Mr J. R. Swingit, who was looking down from his second-floor study window, his eyes like small, ferrety searchlights. The new girl, he thought. Soon have her in shape. Soon make her learn the ropes.

The school reminded Harmony of Dracula's castle. She sensed difficulty and trouble the moment she arrived. She wished she was somewhere else. Most of the kids seemed so much bigger than her, except for a small, tousle-haired girl with strangely haunted eyes, standing in front of her.

'I'm Ellie Burns. I talk too much. Most kids don't like me, but I don't like them either. The school counsellor says I'm her worst nightmare. Who are you?'

'Harmony Parker. Who's that?' Harmony asked, indicating a spotty-faced boy with an ear-ring who was looking at Harmony as if he might squash her like an insect.

'Stub Martin. Eats rats and pulls the ears off baby rabbits.'

'Looks as if he's had his brain removed to make room for more air,' Harmony observed.

'Don't cross him, though,' Ellie warned, 'he makes kids eat earwigs.'

No doubt about it. Things were going to be tough here, Harmony realized. To survive she would need all her wits and deviousness.

She got through the morning without any major disasters, though a dash of bad luck meant that she was in the same class as the bully-boy Stub Martin and he glared at her all morning, trying to intimidate her, she supposed. It was a relief when the bell went for break-time. Hundreds of children swept along the corridors towards the refectory, where there were drinks machines and a table where you could buy crisps and biscuits. The caretaker, a man with a ruined face and the sloping shoulders of the defeated, was scrubbing a new batch of graffiti from the walls — GIVE VIOLENCE A CHANCE; SWINGIT EATS IT: DIE FOR THE GUNNERS. It was a depressing place: peeling, yellowish paint; scuffed floors; furniture that had long outlived its sell-by date; fluorescent lights buzzing overhead.

Harmony stood watching all these strangers and felt ill at ease. If only I had the Queen's Nose, she thought, I'd wish that I could go back to my old school. Then I'd wish . . . her wishing stopped abruptly as she noticed something that triggered a whole new train of thought.

Seated at a table, surrounded by his cronies, was Stub Martin. He was twirling something across his knuckles. A coin. A fifty-pence piece and as Harmony watched, she thought she could perceive a glint from the image of the queen. Her mind raced. The riddle said *One letter away from snub* and that could be Stub. The bell she had heard in Uncle Ginger's shop was like the school bell. Stub had the coin. She was sure of it. There was only one way to find out.

Ellie watched in amazement as Harmony strolled up to Stub to ask him something. No one just went up to Stub Martin without being asked. Not unless you were brain-dead or ill, or if Stub himself had ordered you to approach.

'What is it, squirrel-head?' Stub chortled.

'I need change for a drink. Can I take that fifty pence?' Harmony asked.

Stub's mates watched to see what he would do. He was unpredictable.

'Yeah, you can have it for a quid,' Stub said, with a smile.

Harmony looked at the coin. The Queen's Nose glinted. Was she the only one who could see it?

'All right. Done.' And Harmony held out a pound. Stub took it but closed his fist over the fifty pence. Harmony noticed the ring with a skull and cross-bones on it. She had been right.

'Price has risen in line with inflation,' he said. 'It's two quid.'

'But I haven't got two quid!' Harmony exclaimed.

'Bog off until you have, then,' Stub said to the laughter of his gang.

Fuming, Harmony walked away.

'She must be a few cards short of a deck, Stub. Or maybe she thinks it's magic or something,' said a rat-faced boy with bad teeth.

'Wish it was,' Stub said, idly stroking the edge of the coin. 'I'd wish for the whole place to blow a gaff, then I wouldn't have double chem with old Ma Kermit.'

The bell rang and everyone started to troop off to classes. Stub yawned, tripped over a Year-One girl and knocked a can of Coke over a Year-Two boy, with no idea that upstairs in the chemistry lab his wish was already waiting to begin.

Mrs Commode – Kermit to the children because of her unfortunate resemblance to the common frog – was setting up equipment in the laboratory. It was the lesson she most dreaded. Year Four, Group E, with ten special needs and a psychopath called Stub Martin. And here he was now, with his little gang of followers.

'Sit down, shut up and don't touch the powder in the glass phial,' Mrs Commode said, inviting the opposite to happen, of course. Some people never learn.

Stub sat down and started fiddling with the little phials and gadgets on the desk. To make the others laugh he poured a little scoop of powder into a glass funnel. It foamed and immediately bubbled up and over on to the desk. Stub smirked. Other children giggled. The foam splashed and gurgled and grew at an alarming rate. Within seconds it was gushing on to the floor and still frothing out of the funnel. A few of the laughs became nervous titters, then died. Some children moved towards the door and ran out. Mrs Commode was in the store cupboard, blissfully unaware that her laboratory was starting to turn into a giant bubble bath. Soon even Stub felt nervous, realizing that he was a part of something that was getting out of hand. Then he too ran from the lab.

The foam was nearly two metres high and spilling into the corridor at a frighteningly quick rate. It was strange, sticky, smelly stuff that gurgled with a disturbingly human sound, like a small child being strangled. Nightmarish. A greenish-grey snot colour, and continually multiplying. Osmosis gone mad. And now it was making its way along the corridor, a wobbling, gurgling, jelly-like wall that didn't seem to know how to stop.

Harmony had gone to see her year-group tutor before chemistry, but heard the commotion and dashed into the corridor to see what was happening. Children were running, some sniggering, a few smaller ones frightened. This is true chaos, thought Harmony, with some pleasure. Even then, she had a suspicion that this was no ordinary accident, that something to do with the Queen's Nose lay behind it. Did Stub know it was magic? If so, how did he know? As the foam grumbled towards her she decided it was best to run and think at the same time.

The foam was going in all directions at once. Glugging out of the plug holes of sinks, bubbling up from toilet bowls, terrifying James Whetting, who was sitting on one at the time with his trousers around his ankles. For the rest of his life, poor James Whetting could never go to the toilet without checking the bowl for killer foam first. If anything, the foam seemed to be growing quicker and thicker as it spread. It was now gushing from windows and dripping down the outside walls. Smithers made a valiant last stand with his mop in the refectory, but as the foam lapped his ankles, he dropped the mop and legged it out of the school. He wasn't paid to be a hero.

Mr Swingit had his own private bathroom. A place he often retreated to for a quiet moment. He was in there now, wondering why he wasn't working in a nice, safe, middle-class school instead of this dump full of spotty deadheads and problem children, when he heard the noise outside. Already in a bad mood, this made him furious and he ran into the corridor to see what was going on. Children were running everywhere.

'Stop! No running in corridors, you little animals!' Swingit shouted.

But horror of horrors, no one took a blind bit of notice. What was happening here when he, J. R. Swingit, was ignored by mere children? Children who, as far as he was concerned, had more in common with vegetables than with human beings. Had the whole world gone mad? A horrible burping sound made him turn and he was face

22

to face with a wall of disgusting stuff like creamy whipped mousse made from dead brains.

'How dare you! Get out at once! This is my school! Get out! Stop!' Swingit shouted, with his hand up in a futile King Canute-like gesture.

His nerve failed and he ran into the playground, like everyone else in the school. Or nearly everyone else. Mrs Commode was still trapped, spluttering and coughing, in the chemistry lab.

CHAPTER 3

Harmony looked up at the school building. It needed a good wash, but this was ridiculous. Children cheered as foam started to belch from the chimneys. Mr Swingit stood near by.

'Where did all this start?' he asked.

'Chemistry lab, sir,' said a small boy. 'Mrs Commode's still in there.'

'That's all I need – a dead chemistry teacher. Bang goes my promotion.'

Suddenly a cheer went up as the hopeless Mrs Commode appeared at the school entrance. She was about twice her normal size as she was covered in thick, clinging foam. She wobbled like Mr Blobby towards the unsympathetic Mr Swingit, who ordered some children to hose her down by the bike sheds. By now, the police had arrived and were trying to work out what had happened. The fire brigade were already battling with the foam with high-powered hoses.

Harmony was more interested in the Queen's Nose. She'd had enough of trying to get the coin back from Stub by asking. He was a big lard-ball of a bully but she was determined to get the coin back and now was as good a time as any. Thick as he was, there were too many people around for him to start pushing her around in public. She stood in front of him.

'Stub, you may be front runner in the school zombie competition, but before your brain decomposes completely I want that fifty-pence piece.'

'Dream on, sucker,' Stub replied.

Without warning Harmony flew at Stub, taking him completely by surprise. Girls aren't supposed to do this, he thought as he fell, winded, to the ground. The coin fell and spun to a halt at Mr Swingit's feet a few metres away. Harmony raced over and tried to pick it up but Mr Swingit swivelled his foot over it.

'What is going on?' Mr Swingit asked.

'That coin's mine, sir. I paid Stub Martin for it.'

'Liar! It's mine,' Stub sneered.

Mr Swingit looked with utter contempt from Harmony to Stub.

'Martin, you have much in common with the humble amoeba. Neither of you speak coherently and you barely have a brain cell between you. However, what we are after here is something called the truth. Now, is the coin yours or hers?' Mr Swingit asked.

'It's mine, sir,' lied Stub.

'He's lying. I can prove it's mine,' Harmony said.

'How?' Mr Swingit inquired.

'Look at the coin. The date on it is nineteen eighty-two. I know because my uncle gave it to me.'

'So it has sentimental value?' Mr Swingit asked.

'Sort of,' Harmony said.

Mr Swingit looked at the coin. Nineteen eighty-two. He turned to Stub. He'd been waiting for an opportunity to rid his school of this lout. Now it had arrived.

'You are expelled. Go on, get out,' he ordered.

'I was going anyway,' Stub said with a show of bravado, and glaring at Harmony, he walked away. Harmony didn't feel sorry at all. Stub had asked for it. She held out her hand for the coin. Now it would be hers again, but Mr Swingit put it in his pocket.

'You can claim it tomorrow at nine thirty in my study,' he said.

'But –' Harmony began.

'But nothing. Today I have seen my school filled with foaming muck from hell. It will cost a fortune to clear up, though praise be for insurance policies. You will get your coin tomorrow. Now buzz off before I expel you too.'

Some hope, Harmony thought as she trudged home.

Harmony needed the Queen's Nose back because she wanted to wish for something to help her father and the problems now facing her family. When she telephoned Uncle Ginger and told him about her adventure at school, he pointed out that she could not actually wish for things for herself. The riddle had said of the ten wishes that *they are yours, but then again, not*. Ginger explained that she was the guardian of the coin. She could only help others by wishing for them, or by guiding them in their wishes. The coin was not a personal genie for her own use. She would wait until morning, get back the coin and think how best to use it, especially now that Stub had inadvertently wasted one of the wishes.

Things were definitely getting worse at home. Grandma still refused to acknowledge that Mr Parker actually existed, which made mealtimes tense. Mr Parker had been doing his best to be a house-husband. He planned to start a roof garden where he would grow flowers and vines. Mrs Parker was very worried about him, but did her best to ignore his domestic failures, such as burning holes in clothes when he tried to iron them, turning instant meals into instant disasters and painting the walls of the flat in a vomit orange colour. Mrs Parker and Grandma were snappy with each other and Harmony and Melody took every available opportunity to insult each other. Domestic bliss was a distant memory and the next morning Harmony was glad to slam the door to the flat. At last she would get her coin back.

Mr Swingit sat back in his chair, the old green leather of its seat creaking, though it could have been his knee joints. He brushed a piece of fluff from his charcoal-grey suit and surveyed Smithers the caretaker mopping the last remnants of foam from the floor. The study smelt of polish and disinfectant, because he was always making Smithers clean and polish when no cleaning was necessary. It was the head's way of keeping Smithers in his place. To Mr Swingit's knowledge, Smithers had not said a word since joining the school, which unnerved him, so he took every opportunity available to show who was boss.

'Uppity little oink,' Mr Swingit muttered to himself.

'Pardon, sir?' Harmony said.

He'd forgotten she was there. The new girl. What did she want? Oh yes, that wretched coin. He took it from his desk and held it up. The Queen's Nose glinted, but Harmony was sure she was the only one who could see it.

'When I was a child this would feed a family of five for a month,' he commented, turning the coin.

'Must have been a family on a diet, sir,' Harmony said.

Mr Swingit looked sharply at her.

'The thing is, I don't really like children at all. Does that come as a surprise to you?' he asked.

'Not at all, sir.'

Mr Swingit warmed to his theme.

'Children just aren't useful, are they? I mean, useful like motor vehicles or rain forests or hip-joints.' He took an adjustable spanner, a set of false teeth and a paper guillotine from his desk drawers and placed them on the desk. 'All useful. But children? I don't think so. You see my point?'

'Yes. Very interesting, sir. Can I have my coin back now?'

Mr Swingit's small eyes narrowed as he looked at her. 'What is it about this coin that is so special?'

Harmony decided to tell the truth. Swingit wouldn't believe her anyway, so it wouldn't matter. 'It makes wishes come true.'

'Ha! Wishes stopped coming true years ago. I knew there was no wishing fairy when I was dropped from the first eleven at school for pinching Judith Arkwright's bottom in physical science.' His eyes misted over at the painful memory. 'Education will be the death of me. I wish . . .' and he held the coin in his fingers, 'I just wish my school could be free of children. Now that would be something.'

Harmony was horrified. What had he done? What would happen?

'Nature calls,' Mr Swingit said and left for his private bathroom, after putting the coin in his desk. 'I'll hold on to this. You can have it tomorrow.' He left.

Harmony felt angry and powerless. Smithers stopped his mopping and shrugged his shoulders in a gesture of sympathy. After all, he'd suffered years of tyranny himself from Mr Swingit. He took a key from his pocket, slipped out into the corridor and quietly locked Mr Swingit's bathroom from the outside, then returned. Harmony watched, intrigued. What was going on here? Smithers went to the desk and took out the fifty-pence piece coin and handed it to Harmony.

'Thanks!' she said, amazed. She had another fifty pence in her pocket and gave it to Smithers to replace the real Queen's Nose. Smithers winked and put the replacement

coin in the desk. Things were looking up. She had found
an ally.

Ten minutes later it was break-time. Harmony was in
the refectory chatting to Ellie. There was bustle and noise
and clatter, children coming and going, pushing and shov-
ing. Upstairs there was more clatter as Mr Swingit banged
on the door trying to get out of his toilet. Furious because
there was no toilet paper, he had now found some fool
had locked him in.

'Let me out!' he bellowed.

Out in the corridor Mr Smithers leaned on his mop
and whistled a little tune to himself, as Mr Swingit got
more and more irate. Just when he thought Mr Swingit
was on the verge of a major heart attack, he opened the
door. Unfortunately this was the same moment that Mr
Swingit had decided to barge it down, and he hurtled
through the opening and down the stairs opposite, bump-
ing and shouting as he went.

Harmony couldn't believe it. She had just got a drink
from the machine for Ellie, and turned to give it to her,
but Ellie had almost gone. Only her outstretched hand
remained, waiting to take the drink. Spellbound, Harmony
reached forward and Ellie's hand took the can. As her
fingers closed around it, they started to shimmer, then
disappeared altogether and the can clattered to the floor.
Harmony felt the air where Ellie had been moments
before, but there was nothing, only her school bag on the
floor spilling books and toilet rolls she had stolen from

Mr Swingit's toilet. In fact, everyone else had vanished too. It was like the *Marie Celeste*: half-eaten sandwiches; dropped crisps; cups of hot chocolate still steaming; spilt drink cans; bags and books everywhere, but no children. Except Harmony. The guardian of the coin, she thought. Perhaps that's why I'm still here. But where have they all gone?

That was precisely what Mr Swingit wanted to know after tumbling down the stairs and banging his head on a table. He stood up, brushed the dust from his suit, took a pair of broken glasses from his top pocket and decided that it would not be dignified for a head-teacher to weep. Instead he would get angry. Very angry indeed. He looked around the refectory, wondered where everyone was and decided that he might have a slight concussion and might well murder the first person his eyes rested on just to relieve the tension.

CHAPTER 4

'What is going on?' Mr Swingit asked Harmony.

'You tell me, sir. You had my coin.'

'Don't talk nonsense. I demand to know where everyone is.' Mr Swingit looked under tables, behind doors, under drinks machines. No one. 'Smithers! Come here at once!'

Smithers was in his little room upstairs, having a cup of tea and chuckling to himself at the thought of Swingit stuck in his toilet.

Mr Swingit banged his fist on a table and glared at Harmony, who smiled wanly at him. She was almost enjoying this. She had never seen a grown man go completely bananas and it looked very much as if this might happen. Swingit was going over the top, losing his marbles, heading towards complete dippiedom, and she wanted to watch. She hadn't had this much fun since she'd put a cockroach in Melody's underwear.

Mr Swingit was indeed becoming increasingly crazy, as if two wires in his brain had short-circuited and he was going into overload.

'Where are they?' he roared, looking around wildly. 'Everyone come here right now!'

Silence.

'Right. You are all in detention. Every single one of

you. I am not to be trifled with. All right? Right, then. If you are not all back by the time I count to ten there will be real trouble. One, two, three, four, I'm waiting, five, six, seven, heads will roll, eight, nine, ten! Right. You are all expelled. There.' He looked at Harmony. 'That'll show them. Nobody cuts the cheese around here except J. R. Swingit.'

But where were they? he wondered. What was the point of being in charge if there was no one to be in charge of? He would find them. Wherever they were hiding their miserable carcasses he would find them. This was *his* school and he would stamp *his* authority on it once again. And off he went, up the stairs, looking in each class-room, in the chemistry lab, in the gym, in the library, in the changing-rooms. Where were they? He was gasping for breath. Sweat streamed down his cheeks. He found a few teachers but they pretended not to know what had happened to the children. So they're in it too, Mr Swingit thought. It's a conspiracy and they're all against me. He felt a vein throb in his temple and his throat had become impossibly dry.

This is no good, he thought. I must be rational. Lose my temper and they've won. Be calm. He smoothed his hair, mopped his brow and straightened his tie, talking to himself soothingly. 'I shall not be moved. I shall not waver. They will not win. And when they come back, crawling like insects, they will all rue the day they dared to cross J. R. Swingit.'

By the time he got back to the refectory Harmony had helped herself to school lunch and was scoffing her way through a large plate of chips. Smithers had appeared and was mopping up in a haphazard sort of way. Mr Swingit tried to appear calm and put a little smile on his lips as he approached Harmony. She looked up at him with a bored curiosity. She noticed an ugly vein, like a blue snake, twitching on his forehead.

'Tell me – why is it only you here? To report back to them, eh? Eh? To tell them all how your head-teacher is a nervous wreck? Well, tough luck, young lady, because I am as sane as . . . as a very sane person. So your little game has failed. Hasn't it?'

'Don't know what you're talking about, sir,' Harmony replied.

'Ha! Don't know, eh? Think I'm falling for that "Don't know, sir" routine, eh? Now, you just shoo off out of here. Go on. Out.'

'But where shall I go, sir? I'm the only one here anyway.'

'Go home then. Back to your soap operas and nose-piercing parties. But be here tomorrow for assembly. Nine o'clock. They'll all be back and then you'll see what real discipline is all about. Ha! Yes. Mark my words.' And off he stormed.

Bonkers, Harmony thought. Stark-raving, off-his-chump, daft-as-a-brush, round-the-bend, bonkers.

*   *   *

That night, much against her better judgement and only because there was no one else, Harmony told Melody what had happened at school. Melody scoffed at the news, as she painted her toe-nails a bright scarlet.

'They can't have just disappeared,' she said, 'it's utterly illogical.'

'They did, except me,' Harmony said.

'Just keep taking the tablets. You're such a child. You really believe all this stuff about the Queen's Nose, don't you?'

'I don't believe. I know. You wait and see.'

'I will. If it is true, which it isn't, what do you intend doing about all those missing children?'

'Even as we speak, a plan is forming in the vastness of my brain,' Harmony said.

'We could wait for ever, then,' Melody said, with a smile as sweet as a piranha.

The next morning was very strange. At two minutes to nine Harmony was the only pupil in the hall for assembly. She stood right in the middle and waited. A few teachers entered nervously. Harmony wondered where people go when they disappear. Do they simply stop existing or are they somewhere else, perhaps in another world or dimension, an invisible one? The big clock in the hall ticked two minutes past nine. The doors opened and Mr Swingit entered. He walked to the stage, his footsteps echoing in the large, almost empty, space. There was

35

nothing in his behaviour to suggest anything was wrong.

He turned and faced everyone – everyone being Harmony.

'Good morning, everyone,' he said.

Harmony looked around at the space, then said, 'Good morning, sir.'

'We'll start by singing some awful dirge meant to turn us all into multicultural nonentities,' Mr Swingit continued. He read from a piece of paper. ' "I'd Like to Teach the World to Sing". Mrs Jones, if you please.' He nodded to Mrs Jones at the piano.

Mrs Jones bashed out a few wonky chords and Mr Swingit, Harmony and a few teachers all started to sing in different keys: 'I'd like to teach the world to sing in perfect harmony . . .'

It was truly awful. The song trailed off into a few squeaks. This is ridiculous, Harmony thought. How long is he going to carry on pretending there's nothing wrong?

'There are one or two announcements,' Mr Swingit continued. 'Someone has been stealing toilet rolls from my bathroom again. I expect that person, whoever they are, to confess immediately after assembly. I hope that is understood, Ellie Burns. Good. Two swimming awards this morning. Kylie Thompson for five hundred metres front crawl. Well done, Kylie, you obviously come from a long line of pond life.'

Mr Swingit held up a medal. After a few seconds of silence Harmony clapped.

'And Clem Atkins has done a thousand metres of breast stroke. Excellent, Atkins. If you don't have brains, then sport is certainly a way of crawling out of the gutter.'

Mr Swingit held up another medal and Harmony clapped.

'Mr Trevor on dinner duty. Mrs Commode on library after school. Any other business?'

Harmony put up her hand. Mr Swingit did his best to ignore her but it was difficult, given that she was the only pupil there. Reluctantly he acknowledged her.

'Yes?'

'Sir, don't you think this is a bit . . . silly?'

Swingit exploded. 'No, but I do think it's a plot! You're all in it! But you'll never get the better of me. Never!'

'Try explaining that to them, sir,' Harmony said.

'To whom?' Mr Swingit asked.

Harmony pointed through the window. A crowd of angry people, the parents of the lost children, was advancing menacingly across the playground. A few reporters and photographers accompanied them. Mr Swingit blanched.

'I am not to be disturbed this morning,' he said and left the hall with more haste than dignity.

Things are starting to get very interesting, Harmony thought.

You cannot make five hundred pupils disappear and expect nothing to happen. Of course, Mr Swingit did not yet believe they had disappeared, but he was getting to that point very quickly. The fact that an ugly crowd of a hundred and fifty or so parents was after his blood assisted in this knowledge. He scampered upstairs to his toilet. Smithers was leaning on his mop in the corridor.

'Smithers, on no account let anyone know where I am,' Mr Swingit said, going into his bathroom and locking the door.

Moments later the crowd poured upstairs and along the corridor, much as the foam had done a few days before. Doors were flung open, rooms searched. A large woman with red cheeks and a blue and white spotted dress led the way.

''Ave you seen Swingit?' she asked Smithers. He pointed his mop at the toilet door. ''E's in 'ere!' she shouted and the crowd gathered around the door. Cameras were poised, ready. The large woman tried the door, then banged on it.

'Come out! We know you're in there!' she yelled, her many chins wobbling fiercely.

'Out! Out! Out! Out! Out!' everyone chanted.

Inside, Mr Swingit was sitting on the toilet, his hands over his ears, staring in terror at the door. What would they do to him? Did they have weapons? Surely there were laws against a crowd of ignoramuses tearing a poor head-teacher apart? These questions were nagging him like a nest of toothaches in his mind, beneath which was the uneasy sense that perhaps the wretched Harmony Parker had been right about the coin. Incredible as it seemed, maybe the children *had* disappeared. Blast the girl!

His thoughts were interrupted by more banging on the door.

'Break it down!' someone shouted.

That was it. Mr Swingit decided he had to escape and find Harmony Parker. He would have to climb down the drain-pipe. He opened the window, took a deep breath, told himself not to look down, and stood on the toilet seat. Unfortunately he slipped and one foot splashed down into the water. This was definitely not one of his better days.

Harmony was in her class-room playing with Monty, who had been snuggled down in her pocket. Smithers had just entered and was fixing a broken desk. A knock at the window made Harmony look up. She smiled. Mr Swingit was balanced on the window-ledge outside, looking very sweaty and bedraggled, his tie askew. He made a gesture to open the window. She shook her head. Let him sweat a bit more.

Mr Swingit knocked again, more urgently, and mimed begging. Harmony sighed, got up and opened the window a little. Given that it only opened from the inside, she had the advantage. Mr Swingit tried to push it fully open but it was no good, he was at her mercy.

'Get me out of this. That lot upstairs want my blood. They think I've lost their children,' Mr Swingit said.

'They're right, then, aren't they, sir? You wished them away. Puff. Gone.'

'Was it really that coin?' he asked.

'Yes.' Harmony took the coin from her pocket. 'It magically found its way back to me,' she said.

'Just get me out of it. Bring them back.'

'Not without . . . an agreement,' Harmony said.

'What sort of an agreement?' Swingit asked.

'A binding one. Between you, me and the Queen's Nose.'

'Why can't you be stupid like everyone else? Yes, yes, all right. What do you want?'

Mr Swingit was desperate. He had no choice but to agree. Harmony reminded him of the insurance money for clearing up the school. Since he had made Smithers clear up most of the mess, the money must still be around. She then made her demands, each one bringing Mr Swingit closer to a complete nervous breakdown. First, a school zoo. Second, a free tuck-shop every break-time. Third, pupils get to decorate class-rooms. Lastly, Harmony to be made pupil representative at school governors' meetings.

Mr Swingit argued, he went red in the face, he almost exploded, but eventually he had to accept all of Harmony's demands, with Smithers as witness to the agreement. Harmony held the coin, rubbed the Queen's Nose and wished.

'I wish that everyone comes back.'

She let Mr Swingit into the class-room, then they and Smithers crept down a back staircase, avoiding the mob, to the refectory. It was still empty. Books, bags, drinks, but no pupils.

'I don't understand,' Harmony said. Then she had a thought. 'Perhaps you have to wish them back, because it was you who wished them gone.' She gave Mr Swingit the coin.

'I hate to hear myself say this, but I wish that all the pupils would return,' he said.

Suddenly legs started appearing all over the refectory, some walking, some standing, others sitting or crossed, some, even, with feet tapping. Legs, but no trunks or arms or heads. It looked bizarre.

'Do it again. You've only half wished them back!' Harmony said. 'You've got to mean it.'

'For goodness' sake, I wish that all of the . . . dear children would come back!' Mr Swingit said irritably.

A few heads and arms and bodies began to materialize. Then more and more. Soon, it was as if the disappearance had never happened. Pupils were chatting, laughing, grimacing, walking. The refectory was a buzz of noise. But something wasn't right. Harmony looked around. Something was still missing. Or, rather, someone.

'But where's Ellie? She was here next to me,' Harmony said, turning on Mr Swingit. 'You have to wish her back too!'

'No. Not her. She stays away for good, and I don't think we'll have you on the school governors either,' Mr Swingit said, a glint of malice in his eyes. He could feel power returning to him and he wanted to use it. If this coin really worked the future could be remarkably bright. He could use it to do exactly what he liked. He might even wish himself the Eton job he should have got years ago.

'I'll go and get the mob, shall I?' Harmony said threateningly.

'I have the coin. I'll just wish them away and –'

Before he had a chance to finish his sentence Smithers snatched the coin from Mr Swingit.

'Smithers, you cretin! Give that back to me at once!' Mr Swingit said, holding out his hand.

Smithers looked at the coin in his hand, then at Harmony and she understood. 'You want to wish?' Smithers nodded. He pointed at Mr Swingit. 'You want to swap places with him. Excellent idea! Be my guest.'

Smithers rubbed the coin and closed his eyes. Mr Swingit seemed to fade a little, then come back. Bits of him started to disappear: the left arm, then the right. He panicked. His left leg disappeared, then his stomach. His right knee vanished.

'No! Smithers, you don't know what you're doing. I'll give you a raise. I've always respected you. I'll make you deputy head. You can have my car, my house, my wife . . . Smithers! Have a heart, man!'

His mouth was the last thing to go, still pleading.

As Mr Swingit disappeared Ellie returned.

Smithers now stood in a resplendent charcoal-grey suit.

He looked every inch the head-teacher. Slowly a figure next to him began to form, shadowy at first, then more substantial: Mr Swingit in Smithers' old janitor's coat, clutching an old mop. He tried to protest but his jaw stuck. He couldn't talk. The wish had rendered him speechless. Smithers beamed at Harmony and gave her the coin.

'Thank you,' he said.

'A pleasure, sir,' Harmony said.

'Sir? Yes, I like it. And my first act as head-teacher is to give you all the day off,' Smithers said.

The children cheered and started to leave. Mr Swingit tried to slink away too.

'Not you, Swingit! You can get this place cleaned up, it's a disgrace. And you can start with my private toilet,' Mr Smithers said with great authority.

On the way home Harmony thought that, all things considered, it had been one of her more interesting days at school. She thought of telling her family about it but none of them would believe her. In any case, another family crisis was looming that would require some serious thought and even more serious action.

CHAPTER 5

Mrs Parker and Melody were out job hunting. Harmony was in the bedroom pondering the Queen's Nose. Three wishes were gone. The seven left had to be used wisely. Harmony desperately wanted to use one of them to get her family away from Grandma's flat. Grandma was now talking to Mr Parker. Instead of helping things this only made them worse, because she only acknowledged him to be rude to him. Worse still, she had caught a glimpse of little Monty and spent hours prowling the flat with a mallet with the aim of exterminating the little mouse should she ever catch him. There were mousetraps with cheese all over the place. Already that morning Mr Parker had trod on one and had spent a painful twenty minutes bathing his toe in cold water. Harmony liked to take the cheese carefully then leave a note saying, THANKS FOR THE CHEDDAR, GRANNY or HOW ABOUT SOME CREAM CRACKERS NEXT TIME?, but this only infuriated Grandma more.

Harmony thought of using a wish to leave the flat. If she did make it she knew enough about the Queen's Nose to be aware that they might end up somewhere worse. Also, it could be seen as a sort of a wish for herself and Uncle Ginger had said that she could no longer wish for herself. Something unforeseen might happen, and not for the first time it would seem like the coin had been playing a trick on Harmony. Often, she wondered if the coin had a life or a mind of its own. Anything was possible. Uncle Ginger had taught her that.

She decided to consult Monty but he had nibbled through the bottom of his cage again and gone. Knowing how voracious his appetite was, Harmony assumed he'd end up in the kitchen at some point. She went and listened outside it as Grandma and Mr Parker argued.

'It's a scandal, sending your wife and only daughter out to work. If you were a proper man you'd get off your backside and work yourself,' Grandma said.

'If I could get a job, I would. Audrey and Melody chose for themselves to try and get a job. And Melody is not my only daughter. You have another granddaughter, you know,' Mr Parker said.

'Humph. She doesn't count. She's more a delinquent than a girl. Should have been sent to boarding-school years ago and left there. Instead, she's picked up all your criminal habits.'

'Dorothy, I am not a criminal! I have been falsely accused of a crime!' Mr Parker said, desperately trying not to be baited by Grandma, but losing.

'So you say. No smoke without a barbecue is what I say. Look at you now, thieving!'

'I'm not thieving. I'm trying to make a cake for us all,' said Mr Parker.

'Yes, with my sugar and flour. Ungrateful lot. I'm sick of supporting you. Why don't you buzz off and join the Foreign Legion? That's what criminals do if they've got any spirit. Not hang around a kitchen all day in their pinnies. And there's that mouse again!'

There was a crash that made Harmony wince as Grandma hammered the mallet down on to the cake mix, splattering Mr Parker, herself and the wall with it. Monty, of course, was too quick and smart to get caught.

Harmony hated to hear all this, but there was nothing she could do. She went back to the bedroom and drew endless pictures of Grandma as a natterjack toad, as a bad-tempered old trout with whiskers, as a piranha and as a killer shark. Although she had nothing in principle against these creatures, she made them all look granny-like and evilly ugly. It was a small revenge but it was satisfying. She took out the Queen's Nose and stared hard at it for a few minutes, then put it under her pillow and went out to the roof garden to get away from the horrible atmosphere in the flat for a while. Once Dad's court case was over and he'd been proven innocent, then perhaps life would change, she thought.

When Harmony returned Mrs Parker and Melody were coming in, both looking triumphant. Mrs Parker had just got a job as a traffic warden. Melody had also got a job, but was more cagey about it.

'A model, actually,' she said, when pressed by Harmony.

'What – a model for a Frankenstein doll?' Harmony asked.

'No. It's a sort of post in advertising at a really posh restaurant called Franco's. It will involve meeting people, having a high public profile, because of my looks,' Melody said defiantly.

'You mean you'll scare away customers they don't want,' Harmony added.

'I think it's disgusting,' Grandma chipped in. 'The criminal cooking supper. My own daughter a traffic warden. I shall never be able to hold my head up again at the Women's Guild stud poker rotary.'

Mr Parker stalked away in anger. He was fed up with Grandma. She hadn't let up all day. He went into the girls' room and stripped the beds to wash the sheets. Anything rather than listen to Grandma, but she followed him into the utility room. Apparently, she wasn't finished with him yet.

'How dare you walk away when I'm insulting you,' she said, slamming the door so that Mrs Parker, who was close on her heels, couldn't come in and stop her.

'Mother! Let me in!' Mrs Parker shouted.

'Not until I've told this criminal what I really think of him,' Grandma shouted back.

Still clutching the sheets, Mr Parker turned on her. 'Do you know what you are, Dorothy?'

'Yes. A poor, put-upon, vulnerable, fragile, meek old lady, whom no one appreciates.'

'Fragile? Ha!' scoffed Mr Parker. 'You're about as fragile as a Centurion tank. About as vulnerable as a fifteen-tonne man-eating crocodile. Meek? As meek as Jaws. You are a tyrant, Dorothy. A loose cannon, a cantankerous old bat.'

Grandma was incensed. 'That's it! Show your true colours, Arthur Parker. I always knew you were as common as muck. Never good enough for my daughter, with your drip-dry shirts and your knobbly knees. You're a low criminal. Everyone knows it. And after you're locked up where you belong, if I wasn't such a lady, I'd call you a bum, that's what I'd do. So all the world would know.'

And off she stalked, slamming the door behind her.

Mr Parker's knuckles were white with tension as he gripped the sheets. 'And I wish the world could see you for the crusty old toad you are!' he said.

As he spoke a fifty-pence piece dropped from the sheets. He picked it up. Must belong to one of the girls, he thought. The door burst open and Mrs Parker entered, followed by Harmony.

'Dad, have you seen —? Thanks,' Harmony said as she took the coin.

Supper that evening was a tense affair. Grandma was nowhere to be seen. What should have been a celebration for Mrs Parker and Melody getting jobs was an exercise in damage limitation.

'Don't worry about Grandma, Dad. With any luck someone will mistake her for an ugly, unwashed alien and shoot her,' Harmony said.

'If only we could all stop being so horrible to each other,' Mrs Parker said. 'Where is Mother anyway?'

'Probably gone to shave off her beard. With any luck the water will shrink her and she'll disappear down the plug hole,' Harmony said.

'OK, Harmony. There have been enough insults for one day. I should know, I've both received and issued many of them,' Mr Parker said wearily.

After supper Harmony decided to use a wish for her mother. Mrs Parker had not worked for years and Harmony knew she was worried about it. She went into the bathroom because it was probably the quietest room in the flat, and the only door with a lock. She took out the coin. She rubbed the Queen's Nose and wished.

'I wish that Mum gets on brilliantly with her new job.' She looked at the coin. 'If you could speak to me, I wonder what you'd say?'

She almost jumped out of her skin when, as if in reply, a loud croak came from somewhere in the bathroom. She looked around. Another loud croak. She looked behind the toilet. Nothing. Another loud croak. There in the bath was a very large, squat toad. Harmony looked at it in amazement. How did a toad get to the top flat in a large block in the city centre? And why was it looking at her in that odd way?

CHAPTER 6

'You are the most beautiful toad I've ever seen!' Harmony said, marvelling at the greeny-brown tones of its skin, the watchful eyes, the horned head. 'I'd better get you out of here. If Melody sees you she'll wet herself.'

The toad croaked.

Harmony lifted it up carefully, enjoying the feel of its slightly damp skin, the beat of its heart against her hand. She crept along the hall and into the bedroom. Luckily Melody wasn't there. She looked through cupboards until she found an old aquarium, then put the toad on her bed while she cleaned the glass.

'This'll do for now. I'll keep you next to Monty under the bed. And no noise when sissie's here or she'll have you minced up and down the toilet.'

The toad croaked as if it understood her general drift.

Harmony needn't have worried about anyone discovering the toad that night. The others were too busy combing the neighbourhood for Grandma. They had been to every bingo parlour, betting-shop and French cinema in the area. No one had seen her. It was as if she had simply disappeared. Eventually they went to the police. Mrs Parker told an officer all she could about where her mother might be.

'Has your mother any distinguishing features?' the police officer asked.

'You mean apart from having the worst personality in England?' Mr Parker said, but was silenced by a look from Mrs Parker.

'She's sort of eccentric-looking,' Mrs Parker said.

'And in a bad temper,' Melody added. 'And she hates mice.'

'But not as much as she hates me.' Mr Parker received another angry look from his wife.

'Right,' said the confused policeman. 'So . . . we've got this nutty-looking, mouse-hating old lady who likes gambling and French films.'

'Yes,' Mrs Parker said.

'We'll do all we can. Officially we have to wait twenty-four hours but we'll keep a look-out.'

'Perhaps she's been abducted,' Mrs Parker said.

'I shouldn't think that likely. I mean, who would want . . . ? You know what I mean,' Mr Parker said, to another withering look from Mrs Parker.

The Parkers went home exhausted. Melody was so tired she slept through Harmony's snores, the toad's croaks and Monty's scratching.

The next morning Melody had already left for work when Harmony awoke. She decided to greet the day with music. She plugged in her electric guitar and barked out a few chords. She started to make up a blues song.

'When I woke up this morning my granny she done gone,
Felt so glad about it I celebrated all day long,
Yeah yeah my gruesome granny she ain't here
With any luck she just gone and disappear,
Oh yeeaahhhhhh.'

Harmony stopped. There was another sound coming from beneath the bed. A croaking, protesting, but oddly human sound. It was a small and pathetically angry voice.

'Oi! Oi you! Shut up! Shut up that horrible row! You're making me deaf!'

Harmony listened more carefully, then bent down to look.

'That's better. Now get me out!'

Harmony took out the aquarium containing the toad. Surely it wasn't the toad talking? It couldn't be. Harmony stared at it. The toad stared back.

'What are you looking at, you cretin?' the toad said.

There was no doubt about it. She had a talking toad. And the voice was fainter and croakier, but disturbingly familiar.

'Gran, it's you, isn't it? Somebody must have made a wish.'

'Your father probably. The man is a mistake from start to finish. Now, just get me out of here and back to normal.'

'Another wish gone,' Harmony said. 'That's five.'

'What are you talking about, you stupid girl? Just get me out and make me normal again!'

Harmony suddenly saw an opportunity. Here was

Grandma, the bane of her life, the bane of her father's life, who had shown Harmony nothing but rudeness, suddenly in her power. It was a gift. A beautiful gift from the coin, via her father, whom she guessed must have inadvertently made the wish when he had the coin. Power. There was also the fact that, to Harmony, Grandma was distinctly more attractive as a toad.

'Come on! Get a move on! Do something,' Grandma said impatiently.

Harmony looked thoughtfully at the toad. 'But, Gran, this is an important moment for science. I need to study you for a bit. It could be really significant for the human race which, by the way, you are no longer running in. Hopping maybe, but not running.'

'I'll see you suffer for this,' Grandma said in her little croaky voice.

'Tell me – what does it feel like? Being a toad,' Harmony asked, genuinely curious.

'I am not a toad!' Grandma said, her little horny head pulsing with anger.

'Oh yes you are. Are your senses different? How about hearing?' Harmony tapped the side of the aquarium. To Grandma it sounded like a roll of thunder.

'Stop it!' she croaked.

'Sorry. I suppose you're not a conventional toad. More a sort of mutant,' Harmony said.

'I am not a mutant! I am your grandmother – unfortunately.'

'You and me have got some serious thinking to do. Breakfast, for example. How about if I catch some juicy flies for you? No? A slug? Beetles? A worm? Bugs from the pond? No?'

'I think I'm going to be sick,' Grandma said. 'You're enjoying this, aren't you?'

It was true. Harmony was enjoying it. And she wanted to share her pleasure, so she took the aquarium, containing her grandmother-toad, to Uncle Ginger's shop.

Uncle Ginger was dozing in a hammock, but he opened his eyes and smiled as Harmony entered. He gave a little mocking croak. 'Aren't you going to introduce me to your charming grandmother, Harmony?'

'How did you know?' Harmony asked. Ginger did just know things, but it was always a surprise to her.

'Stop gabbing and change me back, you morons!' croaked Grandma.

'Why change you back at all?' Ginger asked.

'What a stupid question!' Grandma croaked.

'Is it? Didn't you wake up every morning with a grudge against the world? Weren't you in fact a manipulative and embittered woman and haven't you made my poor brother's life a misery, at a time when he's in so much trouble?'

There was a pause.

'Possibly,' Grandma acknowledged grudgingly.

'Definitely, I'd say. I think it's best to leave you as you are,' Ginger said finally.

Grandma started to panic and lost her human voice as she hopped and flapped against the side of the tank, frantically trying to get out. Harmony watched and felt a wave of pity for the feeble struggles of her grandmother. Her mood changed, as Ginger had known it would.

'Look at her. We've got to change her back, haven't we?'

'It's your decision, Harmony. You're the guardian of the coin.'

'Yes, I have to. I just hope she's a bit more human than she used to be when she does change back. Thanks, Uncle Ginger.'

Harmony had left the coin at the flat, so she decided to carry the aquarium back there. In any case, she thought that, as with Mr Swingit's wish, it would have to be reversed by the same person, so that meant her dad wishing Grandma back to normal, or abnormal in her case. It was a hot day and she stopped in a park to have a lolly. She put the aquarium down on a low wall, finished her lolly and closed her eyes for a moment. Then she opened them and picked up the aquarium to leave when she saw that it was empty. She blinked and looked again. Grandma had gone. She searched around, behind the wall, under a nearby bush, but Grandma had gone. She felt her tummy tighten into a knot of panic. Before it had been fun. Bizarre, but fun. This was serious and she realized how the rest of her family must have felt, chasing around the streets looking for Grandma.

'You all right, love?' a passer-by asked Harmony.

'No, I've lost my gran.'

'What was she wearing?'

'Nothing. She was naked.'

'Oh. Easy to spot, then.'

'Yes. And she's very small. She's a toad,' Harmony said.

'Yeah, course she is, love,' said the man, and he walked away shaking his head sadly.

Harmony noticed a large pound near by. She wondered how could she have missed it before. She went over to it.

'Gran? Are you there? Say something.'

Suddenly a cacophony of croaks began. Dozens of toads appeared on lily-pads, on plants, in the water and on the wall. The noise got louder and louder until Harmony thought her ear-drums would burst. It was impossible to tell which was Grandma.

'Gran!' she shouted over the din. 'I'm sorry, Gran. I should have taken better care of you.'

Harmony had an idea. It might just work. It had to work. She ran off as fast as she could. Across the park, through the streets, across roads, weaving and bobbing between cars, never stopping until she got back to the flat. Mr Parker was in and she dragged him out with her. They raced back the way she had come, not stopping until they reached the park again. Harmony stopped for a moment by the pond and caught her breath. Mr Parker was red in the face. He hadn't run like that in years.

'Now, will you explain?' he asked.

'Wish for Gran to come back, Dad. It's our only chance. Here, you rub the Queen's Nose while you wish,' Harmony said as she gave him the coin.

Mr Parker had given up trying to understand Harmony years ago, so he did as she said.

So it was that moments later a very startled Grandma, completely naked, appeared in the pond up to her neck in water. A few bits of pondweed decorated her head.

'Oh! How on earth did . . . ?' Words failed her. She had not a clue about what had happened.

Harmony did a little celebratory dance of joy, passers-by stopped to look and Mr Parker discreetly took off his jacket to drape around Grandma.

Later that evening the Parkers were gathered in the lounge for a celebratory drink. Harmony kept an eagle eye on Grandma and, so far, had to admit that she did seem a bit more human. At one point Grandma even raised her glass, gave a big, bright smile and said, 'It's good to be back.'

The occasion was something of a double celebration because Mrs Parker had given out two hundred parking-tickets that day and had been rewarded with a special commendation by her boss.

The celebration was disturbed by a croaking sound somewhere in the flat. Harmony tried to follow the sound to its source. She found it in Grandma's bedroom. The Parkers all entered to see dozens of excited toads hopping on the bed.

'How utterly disgusting!' Melody said.

'But where did they come from?' Mrs Parker asked.

Harmony realized what had happened. She explained. 'Nothing could stop them getting in. Not at this time of year. Don't you see? It's the mating season. They're all boys, Gran. They're after you!'

CHAPTER 7

As far as Harmony could see, the main thing wrong with Melody was her whole personality. If only that could be traded in for a new one and perhaps if she were given a proper working brain at the same time, then she'd be fine. In the meantime Harmony had to put up with her as she was. That often meant having to deal with her useless boyfriends too. One in particular, Gregory, just would not let go, even though Melody had chucked him months ago. Telephone calls, letters, flowers, cards, but Melody ignored them all. How a person could be broken-hearted over anyone, especially Melody, was beyond Harmony, but there it was. The whole thing was a mystery.

Harmony tried to let Gregory down gently by telling him that Melody never mentioned him, considered him to be an immature dink and wouldn't go out with him again even for a joke, but it didn't work. She also tried telling him the truth about Melody – that she was a stick insect who read the problem pages in dippy girly magazines and who dreamed of new places to use deodorants. Nothing could persuade him. He was still hopelessly in love with her.

However, Harmony made a very useful discovery about Gregory. He was brilliant at maths. He could solve mathematical problems in his head for which most people would need a calculator. She realized she could use this to her advantage, so she did a deal with Gregory: if he did her maths homework she promised to put in a good word for him with Melody whenever possible. It was an arrangement that worked very well for Harmony and she got an A in maths without doing any work at all. After about a month, however, Gregory was becoming less enchanted with the other part of the bargain.

'Are you sure she knows how much I love her?' Gregory asked as they walked back from the Job Centre where he had failed yet again to get a job.

'Of course, and I tell her how brilliant you are all the time,' Harmony lied.

'She hasn't replied to any of my love-letters. I've sent a hundred and seventy-six now,' Gregory said bitterly.

'But that's because she's practically illiterate,' Harmony said. 'Give it time, Grogsy. She'll come round.'

'Oh yes? I just don't trust you any more, Harmony. And anyway, with this glamorous job she's got, there are probably hundreds of blokes after her.'

'Somehow, I don't think so. If there were, she'd be crowing about it, but she's strangely silent about her job. Tell you what – let's go and see.'

'But that would be spying on the woman I love! The woman whose image is marked indelibly on my soul,' Gregory said.

'Not at all, Grogsy. It would be showing your concern for her welfare,' Harmony said.

Twenty minutes later Harmony and Gregory arrived at the restaurant. They both looked at it in surprise. It was a real dive. The sign said Franco's Frisky Fillets and it looked like the kind of place in which you would eat only if you were desperate, your taste-buds had been surgically removed and you had poor eyesight. Harmony looked inside and a man behind the counter, presumably Franco, gave a giant sneeze over a piece of bread he was buttering, then spat on the bread, wiped it on his sleeve and gave it to a customer.

'I thought you said it was glamorous,' Gregory said.

'No, Melody said it was. She often has a difficult relationship with the truth,' Harmony said.

Gregory looked around. There were unemptied dust-bins, rotting fruit and vegetables on the pavements and litter everywhere.

'It's not even in a very nice area. It's all a bit smelly,' Gregory said, then he saw something that shocked him to the roots. 'Oh no!'

Harmony stared down the street to where Gregory was pointing. 'Blimey!'

Melody was walking towards them wearing a large, badly made, plastic fish head and a sandwich board bearing the invitation: GET YOUR CHIPS AT FRANCO'S — THE PERFECT PLAICE FOR FISH. She looked like she felt, extremely silly. A few children were following her, laughing.

'Quick, hide in here!' Gregory said, pulling Harmony into a shop doorway.

'Why are we hiding?' Harmony asked.

'Because she'd be humiliated if she saw us,' Gregory said.

'Yes. So what's your point?'

'My point is – we mustn't upset her!' Gregory said.

'You mean we let her lie her head off about all this glamorous-model stuff?' Harmony asked.

'Well, yes,' Gregory said feebly.

'I knew love was blind. I didn't know it was deaf and daft too,' Harmony said. 'You really are a dipstick in a class of your own.'

Gregory had had enough. 'I don't believe you are trying to help me with Melody at all. And from now on you can do your own maths.'

'Grogsy, come back. I'm sorry . . .'

But it was too late. Gregory strode away.

That evening when Melody came in from work Harmony couldn't resist a few references to modelling being a 'fishy business', especially when the 'chips are down' and you have to 'keep your head'. Afterwards she told Melody how 'board' she was with sandwiches. Melody shot splintery looks at her sister but couldn't be sure that Harmony knew the truth.

Later on, after feeding Monty with some of Grandma's secret store of biscuits, Harmony wanted something to do, given that she hadn't a clue how to do her maths homework. She decided to find Melody and annoy her with a few more snide remarks, because she was irritated by losing Gregory as a homework boffin. Irrationally, she blamed her sister. She knew it was unfair but that was how she felt. She heard Melody talking to a friend on the phone. Harmony crept along the hall to listen.

'I'm just so exhausted, but I have to keep the job because we need the money at home. But it just gets worse at work and from tomorrow I'm serving all day in the café. It's utterly disgusting, I smell like a chip pan. I just wish that some amazing man would come along and save me. A big macho guy on a motor bike or some adorable knight in shining armour. I need a Mr Right.'

Harmony felt guilty. It had never occurred to her that Melody was capable of making personal sacrifices, but here she was, doing a horrible job to help them all, including Harmony herself. OK, if Melody wanted a man to come along and save her, even if it did all sound like some yukky damsel-in-distress story, that's what she, Harmony Parker, would try to provide. With the help of the Queen's Nose, of course.

She went into the bedroom and took the coin from beneath her pillow. This was truly a wish for someone else, she thought as she held the coin and touched the Queen's Nose.

'I wish that Melody's wish comes true and some bloke comes to save her from that rotten job.'

She put the coin back under her pillow. Seven wishes gone now. She suddenly realized that she should have wished that Gregory would be the man of Melody's dreams. That way she might have got him to carry on doing her maths for her. But it was too late now. She'd made the wish. Everything was now up to the Queen's Nose.

CHAPTER 8

Franco's café was a truly awful place. It had a serving bar for the take-away customers and a seated area behind the plate-glass shop-front. The tables were scuffed and had layers of grease and dirt that no amount of scrubbing would shift. The sauce bottles had no tops and so they were covered with a crusty, congealing gunge which was good news for bacteria but bad news for customers. The fat for frying the chips was so old it had a pension. The chips were like over-inflated slugs and a brownish-grey colour. The fish Franco cooked was ninety-five per cent greasy batter and five per cent cod. Dusty jars of pickled eggs and onions were stacked on shelves on the serving counter, with all the sell-by dates long, long gone.

Franco himself didn't believe in culinary hygiene, nor in personal hygiene, to judge by the stained and sweaty old vest he wore stretched taut over his big belly, and his upsetting habit of picking his nose with one hand while frying chips with the other. It was a standing joke among customers that the last time Franco considered brushing his teeth the toothbrush hadn't been invented, so he gave up and never bothered again. Certainly, to stand directly in front of him, especially if he had his mouth open, was to put your health and safety at risk. Small children and even large dogs had been known to faint when confronted with the horror of Franco's breath.

This was where Melody worked. She had dreamed that her first job would be the rung of a ladder that would take her directly to glamour and wealth. What she got was Franco's. The morning after she had been seen by Harmony and Gregory she was trying to serve customers, clean the tables and keep out of Franco's way. A rough-looking group of men at one table kept harassing her and asking for sauce, vinegar, salt, pepper. She was hot and her skin felt like warm treacle from the heat of the cooking. Franco was in a particularly abusive mood:

'Hey, come on, babe. Fred asked for three teas about two minutes ago. You deaf or just stupid? Get a move on, you lazy cow!'

Melody tried to ignore him.

Franco turned to a customer and indicated Melody. 'Can't get decent help these days,' he said. 'Just these moron bimbos. All body and no brains.'

Suddenly, and with absolutely no warning, there was an almighty crash as a 1000cc Harley-Davidson motor bike crashed through the plate-glass window with the roar of a pride of lions and the force of an explosion. Customers screamed and shouted, dived under tables and cowered in corners as glass splintered and showered the whole café. Franco had never moved so fast in his life and dived behind the counter.

The motor bike reared up like a horse, then dropped

down, the powerful engine still turning over. Astride the bike sat an urban warrior: red bandanna, white cut-away vest, oiled shoulders, commando trousers and boots, and all manner of guns and knives. A bandoleer of bullets was fastened across his chest and he held what looked like an anti-tank gun. He also wore in a holster a jagged knife at least thirty centimetres long. Rambo had come to Franco's. Or someone very like Rambo. He even had the Sylvester Stallone lip curl and sneer, visible beneath his Judge Dredd helmet visor. He spoke in a throaty American accent.

'Seems like you punks don't know nothin' 'bout how to treat a lady. All hit the deck. Now!'

A few customers who weren't cowering already on the floor lay down, but a few men were too stunned to do anything but stand and gawp.

'Seems like you punks don't hear good neither,' the stranger said, picking up one of the men so violently that he went straight through the ceiling. Plaster dust showered down on everyone.

'Seems like you punks don't decorate so good neither,' coughed the stranger.

He reached across the counter and hauled the quivering Franco up by his collar.

'You the dog-breath punk who owns this heap of dust?'

Franco was so terrified he could only stutter, 'I-I-I wh-wha, I haven't d-d-done, I m-m-mean it's not f-fair.'

Jars of pickles and eggs fell and shattered as the stranger dragged Franco like a shivering sack right over the counter.

'Ain't fair, huh, punk? Well, I got a message for you, punk. Life ain't fair. 'Bout time you learnt that.'

Franco fainted in terror. The stranger let go and Franco's senseless body thudded on to the floor. The stranger turned to Melody, who was too terrified to scream. He gave her a wry smile.

'Hop on my chopper, babe. I'm takin' you away from all this,' he said.

'I don't want to hop on your chopper! Why are you doing all this? It's horrible,' Melody said, almost hysterical.

Then she stopped. She recognized . . . what was it? Something in the stranger's voice was familiar. With a wave of feeling that was horrified disbelief mixed with relief, she looked at the stranger.

'Gregory? Is that you?' she asked.

As she said his name, something changed in the stranger's demeanour. Whereas he had exuded danger and power a moment earlier, his body now seemed to shrink and shake. He took off his helmet and there was Gregory, looking as surprised as anyone else at what was happening. He looked around as if the carnage had nothing to do with him, as if he was waking from a dream.

'Melody,' he said.

'Gregory! What do you think you're doing?'

'I don't know. I was at home, just sort of dozing and day-dreaming, about you actually, and then . . . I say, who did all this?' Gregory asked, registering the complete destruction around him.

'You are utterly, completely, brainlessly mad. You terrified me,' Melody said.

'Sorry. Suppose I'd better push off, then.'

'Yes. Now. Before the police come and lock you up in a high-security loony bin for demented twits.'

'Right. Sorry. Er, I'm not sure how you ride this . . . bikey sort of thing,' Gregory said as he struggled to wheel the massive machine away.

That evening Melody told her family what had happened. No one believed her except Harmony, who sat entranced. She decided that tomorrow she would spend all day outside the café to monitor what might happen. Probably nothing, but with the Queen's Nose, you could never be sure.

The next morning Harmony hid behind a car and watched the café. It was still a complete mess. Melody was inside sweeping up broken glass and debris. On the pavement were two police cars. A policeman was taking notes while Franco was pointing and gesticulating; he had been in a state of near complete nervous collapse since he had regained consciousness. It was all a mystery. No one seemed to know who the avenging biker was, where he came from, why he did it, and he just seemed to have vanished, as if he never existed.

'I didn't quite imagine it would happen like this,' Harmony said to herself.

'How did you imagine it, Harmony?' Uncle Ginger said.

Harmony was startled by his voice. She looked around but Uncle Ginger wasn't there.

'Here, in the mirror.'

Harmony looked and there in the wing mirror of the parked car was Uncle Ginger's face. 'Uncle Ginger! Hi. I meant that I thought I was helping,' Harmony said.

A woman passing by stopped for a moment to watch this girl talking to a wing mirror, then she hurried on.

'Perhaps you are helping,' Uncle Ginger said. 'That was some motor bike. And fun to see Gregory in action like that.'

'Yes, but it all seems to be getting out of control,' Harmony said, feeling that this conversation was the wrong way round. She should be saying outrageous things and Uncle Ginger, the adult, advising caution and safety.

'What's wrong with you? I thought you were a rebel, Harmony?'

'Yes, but the plan wasn't to destroy a chip shop!' Harmony said.

A man passed by and realized that the world really was mad now that girls were talking to motor cars.

'All I'm suggesting is that a little disorder is not always a bad thing. It can energize things,' Uncle Ginger said. 'After all, out of chaos can come . . . ?'

'Harmony.'

'And she's a good thing. Isn't she?' Ginger said, smiling. 'Uh oh, I think I'm about to leave. Speak to you soon. 'Bye.'

The car started and drove away. Harmony looked back at the café. The police had gone and there was a semblance of order about the place. Glaziers had replaced the large plate-glass window.

'Are you sure you didn't know that maniac?' Franco asked Melody suspiciously.

'Yes. Quite sure.'

'But somebody said you called him Gregory,' Franco persisted.

'I just thought he looked like someone I used to know,' Melody said.

'A likely story. Come on, get a move on and sweep up. Then you can wipe down the tables. And I'm going to dock your wages to pay towards that window,' Franco said.

'But that's not fair!' Melody said.

'Fair! Life ain't fair, girl. About time you learnt that.'

Then, for the second time in two days there was a blinding crash. A knight in full shining armour on a white charger hurtled through the window. Two customers fainted in shock; the rest scattered, screaming and shouting. Glass flew everywhere and it was a miracle no one was hurt. It was as if another time zone had smashed into the café. The beautiful horse reared, its nostrils flaring. The knight, wearing a helmet and visor, held a lance so long it was almost the width of the café.

Melody screamed.

'Oh, no! Not again! *Mamma mia!*' Franco wailed.

The horse calmed down and the knight looked at Franco. He pointed the tip of the long lance at Franco's bobbing Adam's apple. Franco blanched and thought he might have a heart attack.

The knight spoke. 'Methinks, knave, thou art without brain or chivalry. How so if I pluck out thy liver with my lance?'

'Please, please don't, sir. I've got a family and a Maltese terrier to keep. Please don't kill me,' Franco pleaded.

'Thou wert a knave and a scoundrel to this' – and here the knight dismounted and turned to Melody – 'this comely maiden, this thing of beauty, this vision of loveliness for whom men would cross continents and slay infidels. If not thy liver, I shall lop off thine arms and pluck out thine eyes and feed them to my warthog whose name is Barry.'

'I'm sorry. It was only a joke. I didn't mean it. Please. Please,' Franco begged, almost in tears.

The knight lifted up Franco (who instantly fainted) by his collar, then turned and spoke to Melody.

'And you, my lady. Get thy fair haunches up on my steed and I will take thee back to my castle, where I shall adorn thee with laces and silks from the Orient and all manner of things from Marks and Spencer's.'

As he finished speaking there was a loud noise like a blocked drain backfiring and his horse raised its tail and produced an impressive amount of dung. It lay on the floor steaming.

'Er, sorry about that,' the knight said.

'Gregory, is that you again?' Melody asked, suddenly realizing the truth.

The knight took off his helmet and there was Gregory's anxious, bemused face.

'I . . . yes. I think it is. Goodness me. Who did all this?' Gregory asked, unaware that he was still holding Franco.

At that moment Harmony entered, unable to contain her curiosity or excitement any longer. She looked around, wide-eyed and incredulous.

'Wow! This is something else!' she exclaimed.

'What are you doing here?' Melody asked.

'Just passing,' Harmony said innocently.

'Liar! This is something to do with you! You and that stupid coin!' Melody said, at last finding an outlet for the anger that had been boiling up in her ever since she had started this job.

'That's right, blame me. Typical. I wouldn't help you if you were the last, ugliest greaseball on earth. Which you are,' Harmony said.

'Oh! Why is everything so horrible?' Melody said, then turned on Gregory. 'And don't you just stand there. Put him down! He's my boss.'

'Oh! Right. Sorry,' Gregory said, dropping the still-unconscious Franco, who fell with a satisfying plop into the horse dung.

'Sorry,' Gregory said. 'Think I'd better go. It's almost tea-time anyway. Er, I don't suppose there's any chance of you going out with me again?'

'You must be joking!' Melody said.

'Yes. Just a little joke,' Gregory said. Then he glanced at the unconscious owner, said, 'Sorry about the shop,' and wandered out. The horse turned and followed.

'What shall we do with Quasimodo here?' Harmony asked, looking down at Franco.

'I think he's coming round,' Melody said.

Franco slowly, hazily, returned to consciousness. He looked up and said hoarsely to Melody, 'You're fired,' then fell back again.

Melody started to laugh. Small, stifled giggles at first, then louder belly laughs.

Soon Harmony was joining her with great, raucous laughs that made her ribs ache. They looked down at Franco, his head cradled in a pile of horse dung, and they both shrieked with laughter that echoed around the remains of the shop and escaped into the street. Melody had lost her job and she couldn't believe her luck. She was free. She never had to come back to this disgusting café again. So she laughed, and Harmony laughed because it felt good.

They only stopped laughing when they got home. There wasn't much to laugh about there.

CHAPTER 9

Mr Parker's court case was looming like a spectre over the family. Ten days to go before his fate would be decided. Someone had sold confidential information about his clients to rival firms. That same person had also printed and signed phoney share certificates and sold them at a huge profit. Everything pointed to Mr Parker, so he was sacked and prosecuted. He knew he might go to prison, and for a very long time. What would happen to his family if he did?

The only glimmer of hope was a former colleague, Jeremy, who alone supported Mr Parker, and publicly stated so, even though it could have affected his own career. He visited Mr Parker with some good news. The whole family, apart from Grandma, who was playing poker with some friends, sat in the lounge to listen.

'I've been able to persuade Sir Anthony Snouch to act as your barrister. Top man. Just back from ten successful years in the States. Never lost a case.'

'But won't he cost a fortune?' Mr Parker asked.

Jeremy smiled and Melody thought what perfect teeth he had. 'Yes, but he owes me a favour. It should be ten thousand, but I'll see what I can do.'

Harmony couldn't bear to see Melody go into her

girly-girly, flirty-flirt act. It made her want to roast her sister on a spit. Very slowly. She started to flick through a magazine. Anything to avoid having to watch Melody. She did a crossword, then noticed a Mum of the Year competition. The first question was, 'Does your mum always listen to your problems?' No, never, Harmony thought, so she wrote down, 'Yes. Always.' The next question was, 'Is she a reasonable and calm person?' Harmony thought that her mum was a hysterical nut, but she wrote, 'Yes. She's almost a saint.' She was about to read what the prize was, when Jeremy said something that caught her attention.

He said he needed an assistant.

'I've always wanted to be a PA,' Melody said.

'You mean Prats Anonymous,' Harmony said.

Melody shot an icy look at Harmony. Their recent moment of reconciliation in the café hadn't lasted long.

'Would it involve a clothes allowance and trips abroad with you?' Melody said, fluttering her false eyelashes at the embarrassed Jeremy.

'No, more accounts work. I need someone with a keen mind for figures.'

An idea immediately sprang to Harmony's mind. 'I know someone who's the absolute dog's dinner when it comes to numbers. He's a genius.'

'Tell him to give me a call, then,' Jeremy said.

★   ★   ★

So Gregory was given an interview and, miracle of miracles, Jeremy gave him the job. He and Harmony shared a Coke and hotdog in the park to celebrate.

'I can't believe it,' Gregory said. 'Thanks.'

Gregory appeared to have only a dim memory of what happened in the café; nevertheless, after those extraordinary events he seemed more confident. Getting this job would certainly boost his confidence even more. Considering what a div he used to be, Harmony thought it was a remarkable improvement.

'Maybe Melody will go out with me again, now I'm a proper business-type person,' Gregory said.

'Forget it, Grogsy. Melody's brain only has room for one thought at a time, and you're not it,' Harmony said, thinking that brutal honesty was probably the best approach, especially as Melody seemed to have gone all soppy over Gregory's future boss. She considered that this was not the most appropriate time to tell Gregory about this. Best not to murder your boss before you even start the job.

'I hope your dad didn't mind me getting a job at his old firm. I mean, with him being thrown out of there and everything,' Gregory said.

'I think he's too worried about the court case to get miserable about anything else. And Mum's exhausted. Now Melody's out of work Mum's having to do double shifts.'

'Sounds like your whole family could do with a break,' Gregory said.

'Oh yeah. What with – peanuts?'

'You can always wish,' Gregory said.

'You don't know how right you are, Grogsy,' Harmony said.

'By the way, Harmony.'

'What?'

'Now I'm a working man I'd prefer you not to call me Grogsy.'

That night while Melody was in the bathroom washing her hair Harmony took out the Queen's Nose and wished.

'I wish, I wish for a holiday so that Mum and Dad can have a rest. Oh, and loads of dosh to pay for that lawyer would be all right too.'

She wondered if that counted as two wishes. She'd have to wait to find out.

Harmony didn't have to wait long because the next morning a letter arrived for her mother:

Dear Mrs Parker

After serious consideration the judges have voted for you as Mum of the Year. You have won a Mystery Adventure Weekend for your whole family, plus the opportunity to win a bonus cash prize.

Congratulations!

Mrs Parker read it again. Then Mr Parker read it. The letter seemed genuine enough and when Harmony confirmed that she had entered her mum for the competition, they all got excited.

'Oh, Arthur, we could go this weekend. It will do us good to get away before your court case. Please,' said Mrs Parker.

'We all need a break. Yes, let's do it!'

'Excellent!' Harmony said.

Mrs Parker read the details. 'It says to be prepared for anything. What on earth shall we pack?'

When it came to meet the coach all of the Parkers had prepared for a completely different kind of weekend, each according to their own fancies. Mr Parker wore little German leather shorts and rock-climbing gear. Mrs Parker imagined a weekend of ballrooms and cocktails, so she wore an elegant red gown with a sash and a large brooch. Melody wore shades and tight satin pants, thinking they would be at a celebrity holiday haunt. Harmony was dressed in SAS army gear, with a fully packed utility belt, as if she was going to war.

The coach arrived. The sign on the front read: NOWHERE. The Parkers were the only passengers. Harmony had the uneasy feeling that something strange was going to happen on this trip.

Two hours later the coach was grinding along a bumpy track that had never been built to take coaches. Branches battered against the sides and windows. Overhanging trees brushed the roof, so that from the inside it sounded as if someone were sweeping the roof. The weather had become gloomy too. Great swirls of dark cloud moved ominously across a grey sky. It started to rain.

Suddenly the coach stopped. The Parkers got out with their luggage and the driver pulled away quickly. The wind was scudding leaves in little brown eddies and branches were creaking so much it seemed the trees were having some ancient conversation only they understood.

Before the Parkers was the Grand Hotel.

'The only grand thing about it seems to be that it's been grandly neglected,' Mr Parker said, wishing he wasn't wearing little shorts as his knees were getting distinctly chilly.

'Transylvania,' Melody said.

'I was expecting something . . . different,' Mr Parker said.

The whole building was covered in ivy and the forecourt was a jungle of weeds. The windows were all dark, mostly cracked and some missing. It appeared to be uninhabited. Two stone gargoyles perched by the front door.

'I think it's cool,' Harmony said. 'Really bad! Sort of place where girls with mousy hair and air bubbles for brains get strung up and tortured. Get my drift, sissie?' Harmony said.

'Girls! Just try to pretend you're human beings for once,' Mrs Parker said.

'I suppose we'd better go in,' Mr Parker said in the tone of one who very much did not want to go in. As they approached Mrs Parker could have sworn that one of the gargoyles winked at her, but she quelled the bubble of hysteria in her stomach.

At the front door Mr Parker pulled an old bell chord, which collapsed into a heap of dust in his hand. Then the door slowly creaked open.

'Mum, I'm scared. What shall we do?' Melody asked.

'Go in, of course,' Harmony said.

CHAPTER 10

Reception was a hall of shadows and whisperings, with doors leading from it and a staircase curling away upstairs. It was gloomy, foreboding. A bat flew across the ceiling and disappeared.

'What was that?' Melody asked, terrified.

'Cool! A bat,' Harmony said. 'Probably a British pipistrelle but we can always hope it's a vampire. You should get on well with it, sissie. And don't worry, they only eat human flesh, so you're quite safe.'

'I just wish I'd been an only child,' Melody hissed, forgetting her terror momentarily.

Candles suddenly lit up, startling them.

'Arthur, there's been some terrible mistake. Call a cab and let's go home,' Mrs Parker said.

Mr Parker picked up the telephone but the wires had been cut long ago.

'No mistake, I assure you. Everything is in perfect disorder,' a grave and doom-laden voice said.

Melody nearly shot through the roof and even Harmony's heart leapt. They all turned to see a huge shadow on the wall and across the ceiling at the top of the stairs, distorted by candle-light. The figure descended and stood before them.

'D. Gallows, head butler, at your service.'

Gallows was dressed in an old-fashioned frock-coat and had the slow, deliberate demeanour of a Victorian undertaker. A permanent hint of a smile that never quite materialized suggested that he was always enjoying some private joke. His face was chalk white, as if he had been dead for years, but nobody had informed him.

'Where did you come from?' Harmony asked.

'Originally, Eastern Europe, but more recently, the kitchen. Cook will prepare you an excellent supper, Harmony. What would you like?'

'Er, fish and chips, please. How did you know my name?'

'It's my job,' Gallows said. He took the rest of their orders for supper. 'Please go to your rooms now. Everything is prepared. Upstairs.'

They all looked upstairs, and when they looked back, Gallows had vanished.

'I want to go home,' Melody said.

'This is brilliant! This is the adventure! Don't you see?' Harmony said, full of excitement. She raced upstairs.

'Harmony!' Mrs Parker called, but there was no stopping her. They could only follow.

They walked along corridors with dancing lights, past statues that looked as if they had once been alive and were now mummified into eternal watchfulness.

The bedrooms had name-plates on them, one each for

the girls and one for Mr and Mrs Parker. The rooms were amazing. Each was created according to the personality or interests of the guest. Melody's was full of flowers and perfumes, with engraved hearts on the walls and a luxurious bathroom with a bubble bath already running.

Mr and Mrs Parker's room had a medieval theme. The walls were decorated with crests and tapestries of jousting and dancing. A disturbingly real-looking model of a jester acted as one of the bedposts. Various weapons hung on a wall and Mr Parker immediately took down a sword so heavy he had to hold it in both hands. He twirled it a few times until Mrs Parker told him to stop being silly and put it away.

Harmony's room had a fairground theme. Bright murals of helter-skelters and ghost trains adorned the walls and ceiling. The bed was a converted dodgem car. A working model of a fun house with a distorting mirror in it stood by the window. Harmony thought it was brilliant. She sat on the bed and took out her Queen's Nose coin.

'Thanks,' she said to it.

'But don't believe everything you see,' Uncle Ginger's voice replied.

Harmony looked around and Ginger's face was fading in and out of the distorting mirror. One moment he had a ridiculously large nose and tapering chin, then the top of his head ballooned into a grotesque swelling.

'Uncle Ginger! You look dead funny.'

'Be careful, Harmony. There's something evil here,' Ginger said, then his voice and face faded completely. Evil was a pretty strong word. Harmony couldn't remember Uncle Ginger ever having used it before.

An hour later the Parkers went down to dinner. They were all dressed elegantly except Harmony, still in her army gear.

The dining-room was vast, with just one table in the centre. Around the room were statues holding candles and in a gallery minstrels appeared and disappeared, accompanied by snatches of music. A large bookcase lined one wall. A huge portrait of a queen overlooked everything. None of the Parkers noticed that her eyes were alive and followed their every movement.

They sat at the table, apprehensive and self-conscious, apart from Harmony, who was enjoying every moment. Gallows entered and flicked out a table-cloth, which showered everyone with dust. Then he placed a plate covered with a silver dome in front of each guest. He bowed stiffly and left.

'What a creep! Still, fish and chips,' Harmony said. She lifted the silver dome and underneath it was a goldfish in a bowl and a raw potato. 'What?'

'That's not . . . ?' began Mrs Parker.

'Yes it is. Do-it-yourself fish and chips. Extraordinary,' Mr Parker said.

'Utterly disgusting. I ordered Coronation Chicken,'

Melody said, lifting her silver lid to reveal a live chicken wearing a crown. She screamed. Harmony laughed. The chicken squawked, jumped off the table and clucked away.

'Oh, I wanted to keep her,' Harmony said.

Mrs Parker turned pale. 'Arthur. We ordered . . .'

'I know. Toad-in-the-hole,' Mr Parker said.

Harmony lifted his lid and there was a plate with a hole in the centre with a toad sitting in it. 'Like Gran,' she said.

Melody felt sick. Mrs Parker felt close to fainting and Mr Parker decided never to eat out again. Harmony was intrigued – whoever was doing all this, whether it was just Gallows or someone else, was going to a great deal of trouble to frighten her family. She wondered why.

There was another small covered plate in the centre of the table. Harmony lifted its lid and there was an envelope addressed to the Parkers. They decided to go back to Mr and Mrs Parker's room to read the note inside it and to eat the emergency supplies which Harmony proudly produced from her army survival belt. As they left the dining-room Harmony was sure she saw the eyes of the queen in the painting flicker.

'The mystery prize is . . . I don't believe it,' Mrs Parker said.

'What? Come on, Mum,' Harmony said.

'Ten thousand pounds.'

'Let me see that,' Mr Parker said.

It was true. The prize was ten thousand pounds, exactly the amount needed to pay for Mr Parker's barrister, Sir Anthony Snouch. Harmony realized that the two wishes she'd made were being counted as one – the odd experience of being at the Grand Hotel.

The note stated that they had to go on a quest to find the prize-money, and that if they failed one of them would end up staying at the hotel for good. Although this was an unnerving thought, none of them really believed it would happen. There was a riddle which provided a clue in the first stage of the quest:

> *Ten to one, and twice in one,*
> *The hunt has now begun,*
> *Find me soon, be very quick,*
> *I are waiting, that's the trick.*

None of them could make any sense of it. Harmony said that if thinking alone couldn't help, then they should look around, in the hope that they might see something that would help.

They formed two search-parties. Mr and Mrs Parker went one way down the corridor outside their bedrooms, and Harmony and Melody the other way. Everything that could possibly happen to frighten them did so. Statues appeared to wink or move. Lights went on and off. Suits of armour clanked. Shadows danced and cobwebs floated magically through the air. Melody opened a door and screamed when she saw a ghostly version of her mother in bed. It was all very scary, but almost too scary, Harmony thought. There is something very deliberate in all this, as if someone is going out of their way to distract us from solving the riddle. She felt less frightened after deciding that someone had planned all this. Everything seemed less scary now.

They reached reception. A grandfather clock chimed eerily, but when Harmony looked at it the hands were stuck at ten to one. Clocks didn't chime at ten to the hour.

'Ten to one. That's what the riddle said: *Ten to one.*'

'*And twice in one.* Meaning what?' Melody asked.

Harmony thought hard. 'Twice in one! The clock is right twice in a twenty-four-hour day. See? Ten to one in the afternoon and then again in the early morning.'

'You're right,' Melody said. 'What about the rest? *I are waiting, that's the trick.* What trick? Clocks don't play tricks, they . . . Hey! Suppose *are* really means the letter R. Take that away from trick and you've got . . .'

'Tick!' Harmony said.

She moved the hands of the clock. A panel in the clock opened to reveal an envelope marked CLUE NUMBER TWO.

'Yo!' Harmony said. 'If you've got a brain, why haven't you been exercising it all these years, sissie?'

She opened the envelope and read the clue:

You have got one, now here's two,
As most people have, that's nothing new,
Let us see what we shall see,
You'll get there if you follow me.

Neither of them could make head nor tail of it. They went back to meet Mr and Mrs Parker, then to bed. Harmony dozed fitfully, the riddle turning over and over in her mind, but eventually exhaustion took over and she fell asleep in a torrent of dreams in which she was trying to get away from D. Gallows, but wherever she turned, he was there.

CHAPTER 11

The next morning Harmony found Melody seated before her mirror putting on layers of face make-up.

'Trying to make the best of a bad job?' Harmony inquired.

'I look awful. Like some horrible painting of a zombie or something,' Melody complained.

'That's a bit unkind to zombies, isn't it?' Harmony said, bouncing on the bed. Then she stopped. 'That might just be it!'

'What might be what?'

'A painting. The riddle. It talked about having *two* then about seeing. Get it? Two eyes. And I was trying to think of all the things that have eyes.'

'And . . . ?' Melody asked.

'Paintings. Have you noticed how weird the eyes are in that painting of the queen? Come on!'

In the dining-room they looked at the portrait of the queen. Painted eyes had been stuck to the eye holes from behind. They looked spooky because they clearly didn't match the face and were more like wide cartoon eyes, looking sideways at a wall.

Melody and Harmony approached the wall. The only thing on it was a piece of paper headed FIRE REGULATIONS.

'Just the fire regulations and a blank wall,' Melody said.

'I know I'm right!' Harmony exclaimed.

'Not unless there's a fire somewhere,' Melody said. She started to read the regulations. 'Hang on. These aren't proper regulations. Listen. "No, they aren't proper at all. Well done. Here's the last clue: *If you're clever and can read, you should find all you need.*"'

'Read what?' Harmony asked. 'Magazines? Recipes? Instructions?'

'Or books?' Melody suggested.

They both turned to a bookcase on the other wall. They went over to it and looked at the titles.

'So, what now?' Melody asked.

'It said, *If you're clever and can read*. There's something here we should be looking for. Something special,' Harmony said.

'Look!' Melody took out a book entitled *Understanding Melody*.

As she did so Harmony heard Uncle Ginger's voice whisper in her ear, 'Beware!'

'Melody! No! Put it back!'

But Melody had opened the book and as she did so the bookcase and the bit of floor on which she stood revolved very quickly and she disappeared behind the wall. Another bookcase was now in its place.

Harmony banged on the bookcase. 'Melody! Can you hear me?'

Nothing. It was as if Melody had never existed. Harmony pushed and shoved, trying to move the bookcase, but it was fixed. She couldn't even see the join where it revolved. After ten futile minutes of shouting and pushing, she went to find her parents.

'My own daughter stuck goodness knows where. When I get hold of whoever is responsible I'll wring their necks. I suppose it's that Gallows creature,' Mr Parker said.

For some reason he was wearing his climbing outfit. Harmony didn't even bother to ask why. If it made him feel better, then good luck to him.

'Arthur, mind your blood pressure,' Mrs Parker said, touching his arm. 'You know what you're like when you get all worked up.'

'Let's go!' Mr Parker said, and strode down to the dining-room.

Mrs Parker looked at Harmony, who just shrugged and ran after her father.

The three of them checked the bookcase again. There didn't appear to be any way of making it open.

'Stand back!' Mr Parker said.

He swept the books off the shelves, then took the hammer from his climber's belt and started battering the bookcase. Wood splintered as he knocked a hole right through. Harmony was amazed. This was a side to her father she had never seen before. What she didn't know was that all the frustration and anger he had felt about losing his job and having to go to court was coming out in the attack on the bookcase. Also, of course, there was the simple fact that his daughter was in danger and he was going to trample anything or anyone that might hamper him from getting her back.

'Go for it, Daddio!' Harmony shouted.

'Whack it harder, Arthur. Never mind your blood pressure!' Mrs Parker enthused, now she realized Melody really was in danger.

Mr Parker stood back and booted the shelving, which shattered and gave way. He walked through the gap, followed by Mrs Parker and Harmony. It was suddenly freezing cold and dark. Harmony took a torch from her belt, feeling pleased that her army gear was proving to be so useful. She switched on the torch just in time. It revealed they were all about to step into a large hole.

'Melody!' Mrs Parker shouted.

'Melody! Melody! Melody!' echoed everywhere.

Harmony shone the torch down the hole. Some six metres below Melody lay on a stone floor. At first Harmony thought she might be dead, but she moved a little and looked up.

'Help!' she whispered. Hundreds of echoes of 'Help!' flew like bats around the walls.

Mr Parker discovered a beam across the ceiling. He took the climbing rope from his belt, looped it around the beam, then tied it around his waist and lowered himself slowly down to Melody.

'Be careful, Arthur, and watch out for spiders!' Mrs Parker said. 'He's terrified of them, you know.'

'He's not rescuing a spider, Mum, though I can see the resemblance.'

Down below, Mr Parker tied the rope around Melody's waist and helped her up. Mrs Parker and Harmony pulled until Melody was safely with them, bruised and shaken, but otherwise unharmed.

'Look at the state of me!' Melody moaned.

'Yeah, but let's get Dad back before we discuss your wardrobe,' Harmony said. Mrs Parker checked the rope around the beam. She took it off for a moment, but slipped on the damp floor and let go. All the rope tumbled down into the hole.

'Oh dear!' she said.

'Nice one, Mum,' Harmony said. 'Now Dad's stuck.'

'Can't we use anything else?' Melody asked.

'There must be something. This! I knew this stupid dress would be useful for something,' Mrs Parker said, and unrolled its long scarlet sash. The sash was perfect. They tied it around the beam, threw the other end down to Mr Parker and a few breathless minutes later he was up with them. They went back into the dining-room and brushed the dirt and cobwebs from them.

'What a place!' Mr Parker said.

'The sooner we leave the better,' Mrs Parker said.

Harmony noticed an old leather-bound book on the floor with the others. She picked it up. The title was *The*

Queen's Nose. Weird, she thought, and opened the book. It had been hollowed out and inside was a large wad of banknotes.

'Look! The jackpot!'

They all looked at the money. Mr Parker flicked through it. 'There must be close to ten thousand pounds here!' he said.

'Just what we need to pay your lawyer, Dad!'

'But we can't take this money,' Mrs Parker said.

'Yes we can. It's the cash prize. We won it fair and square!' Harmony insisted. Also inside the book was an envelope. Mr Parker opened it and read it aloud:

If you are reading this, congratulations, you have won. However, next week, the last laugh is on you. You will lose your court case and go to prison for at least five years.

Yours respectfully

D. Gallows

The next morning on the coach going home the Parkers were very quiet.

CHAPTER 12

The wretched Mr D. Gallows was right. The verdict was announced. Guilty. There were gasps and mutterings all around the court. Everyone was there, including Jeremy and Gregory. Mrs Parker fainted. Grandma was furious. Harmony shouted 'No, Dad, it isn't fair! It's a cheat!' A court official told her to keep quiet or she'd be thrown out.

Mr Parker went a deathly pale.

They had paid Sir Anthony Snouch ten thousand pounds. He had assured them Mr Parker would be acquitted. 'Cut and dried,' he'd said confidently. 'The man's innocent.' And now it had all gone wrong. The court rose for the judge to pronounce sentence.

'Arthur Parker, you have been found guilty of two serious crimes and have set an atrocious example to others. I sentence you to five years in prison, to commence immediately.'

Mr Parker was led away.

Harmony took her Queen's Nose coin from her pocket and placed it on the shelf in front of her. How could she use it? What could she do?

'I wish the world could see you for what you are!' shouted Grandma. 'A bunch of animals and old birds!' She slammed her fist down on the bench where the coin was.

As she left the court, Harmony looked back and saw that the judge had turned into a sheep, the jurors into chickens and geese, and that Sir Anthony Snouch had turned into a pig and was snuffling around. Another wish gone. Could anyone else see this? Harmony didn't know. She didn't care. Her dad was going to prison. He wouldn't see the flowers on his roof garden. He wouldn't be there to nag at Harmony when she did yet another thing to annoy him. The clerk, an elderly man, seemed to be the only one not to turn into something else. He sighed wistfully and tried to say something to Grandma, but she shrugged him off.

They went home to the flat. No one was hungry. Everyone was still in shock. Melody telephoned Jeremy that evening and thanked him in her gushy way for his help, but Harmony could hardly be bothered to mock her.

The next few days went by in a nightmare of numbness. A hint of hope came from an unexpected source – Gregory. He telephoned Harmony and spoke in quick, hushed whispers, telling her to meet him outside his office that evening.

Outside the mansion block Melody was sitting in Jeremy's car. She had been to his office to thank him yet again for the help he'd given during Mr Parker's trial, and Jeremy offered her a lift home, as she knew he would. She was desperately trying to get him to ask her out, using everything she knew: subtle hints, unsubtle hints, coyness, flirtation. Passing the car as she left to meet Gregory, Harmony leaned close to the windscreen and pulled a horrendous face.

'Wasn't that Harmony?' Jeremy asked.

'Yes. We're all very disappointed. Brain surgery is such an uncertain business, and she hasn't responded at all,' Melody said bitterly. Harmony had ruined her plans. As she left the car Melody noticed a folder on the back seat with ROSEBUD written on it.

'What a lovely name,' she said.

In his office Gregory switched on the computer, loaded it, and showed Harmony some files. One was called ROSEBUD. Although he couldn't access it, because it had a secret code-word, the file expanded or contracted each month by exactly the same amount that another file, PARKER, also did. The conclusion: someone was copying Mr Parker's file each month. But why? Unless they wished to do something with the information, like sell it to rivals, perhaps? Gregory said he would try to get into ROSEBUD, then they would know for sure.

They had a lot to think about. As they left the office building, they were busy chatting about what it might all mean, and who might have done it. Neither of them noticed they were being watched. Jeremy had driven back to the office to do some overtime. He wondered why

Harmony and Gregory should be coming out of the building so late. There was one person who might tell him about Harmony. He lost no time in telephoning Melody and suggesting they go out for a meal. She instantly entered a state of bliss. She felt guilty because it didn't seem right to be so happy about anything now her father was in prison, but she knew he would want her to be as happy as she could. Already she started seeing wedding videos in her mind's eye.

The next morning a hand-posted letter plopped through the letter-box. Melody picked it up. On the front was a picture of a rose and someone had drawn a heart around it.

'Rosebud,' Melody said to herself. She opened the letter and read:

> I fell in love with you at first sight. Age doesn't matter, so please, please, say you'll marry me. Your ardent admirer,
>
> XXXXX

'He loves me,' Melody whispered to herself.

Melody spent the rest of the day in the bathroom. When she emerged she was dressed to kill: the shortest skirt in the world; a low-cut silk blouse; high heels; so much eye make-up that she resembled a panda bear. Harmony looked at her and giggled. Mrs Parker was horrified.

'Melody, is that you?' Mrs Parker asked.

'You don't think I'm overdressed?' Melody asked.

'You mean you've dressed? That's not a frock, it's a handkerchief!' Harmony said.

'I'm going to a restaurant with the most gorgeous man in the world, who just happens to be utterly in love with me,' Melody said.

'Who?' Mrs Parker asked.

'Jeremy,' Melody said.

'She was practically snogging him all over his steering-wheel yesterday. He looked terrified,' Harmony said.

Mrs Parker was shocked. 'Melody, he's older than you and he's your poor father's ex-colleague. You can't go out with him.'

'I'm not a child. I can decide for myself,' Melody said petulantly, and strode out.

'Melody! Oh dear. Harmony, I don't think I should tell your father about this when I visit him,' Mrs Parker said.

CHAPTER 13

In the restaurant Melody wanted to talk about their wedding but Jeremy seemed to want to talk about Harmony. It was most annoying.

'I don't know why Harmony went to your office. What does it matter?' Melody asked, pouting her best pout.

'She's your sister. With all the recent trouble at work, I thought you might be concerned.'

'Well, I'm not. And by the way, the answer is yes. Yes, yes, a thousand times yes. I will.'

'Yes what? You will what?' Jeremy asked, confused.

'You tease!' Melody said, playfully squeezing his hand. She imagined a large terraced house in London, a cottage in the country and a holiday villa in Tenerife with a kidney-shaped swimming-pool. Yes, she was going to be very happy with Jeremy.

After Jeremy had driven her home, Melody found Mrs Parker waiting up for her.

'You can't marry him. You're far too young. You're still my little girl,' Mrs Parker said.

'But I am going to!' Melody said. 'He thinks I'm glamorous and intelligent and wonderful, otherwise why would he have written asking me to marry him? Mum, he'll give me my own bank account and everything. I can take you shopping at Harrods every day.'

'Melody, this has got to stop. I forbid you to see him,' Mrs Parker said.

'Tough!' Melody said.

Listening outside the door, Harmony looked at little Monty, whom she was stroking. 'Pass the sick bag, Monts, sissie's in love with a walking bank account.'

The next day Harmony took Monty to Gregory's office because he had managed to break into the ROSEBUD file. With a little triumphant smile he pressed a few keys. To their mutual surprise, however, what came up on the screen was not financial information, but love-letters, scores of them.

Harmony read bits aloud: 'Dear Rosebud, each time I close my eyes I think . . . blah blah blah . . . You are my . . . blah blah blah . . . Your loving Jeremy. Yuk! They go on for ever,' Harmony said, disappointed.

'Funny, though, they take up a different amount of space than they did,' Gregory said. 'I bet he's taken off what was on there before. Swapped it for this stuff.'

'Why?'

'Because he didn't want anyone to read it. Maybe he's suspicious. Cor! Some of it's pretty steamy stuff. Wonder who these letters are to?' Gregory asked.

'Ah, you're not going to like this, Grogsy,' Harmony said.

He didn't. He hated it. He wanted to murder Jeremy and that's what he set off to do. He knew where his flat was and that's where he was going. Harmony followed, pointing out the perfectly obvious fact that if Gregory did murder Jeremy they'd never find out who committed the crimes for which Mr Parker was now in prison. Also, Gregory himself would go to prison, and that would be a fat lot of good to them all.

By the time they reached the flats where Jeremy lived, Gregory had cooled a little, and they decided they needed proof. Hard proof. And the only way to get it was to enter the flat. Jeremy's car wasn't there, so they assumed he wasn't in. The flats had a doorman who sat inside the entrance behind a bank of security screens.

'How do we get past him?' Gregory asked.

Harmony looked around. A little boy with a cheeky face, wearing a baseball cap, was standing a few metres away. Harmony asked him if he wanted to earn a pound. His eyes widened. Minutes later the doorman was disturbed by a banging. He looked up to see a small boy in a baseball cap throwing a ball at the front window. The doorman raised his hand to tell the boy to get lost, but the cheeky lad poked out his tongue and rolled his eyes. The doorman went to the entrance and chased the boy a little down the road.

This gave Harmony and Gregory just enough time to get inside and for Gregory to skim through the computer at the desk to find out the entrance code to Jeremy's flat.

Five minutes later they were in the flat. They didn't know exactly what they were looking for, but at least they were doing something. Harmony felt nervous. They were breaking the law. They were seriously breaking the law. However, when she thought of her dad in prison she felt fine about being in someone else's flat, looking through their things. Then, behind a picture in the bedroom, Gregory found a wall safe. He tried all the numbers he knew that had something to do with Jeremy in order to discover the right combination to open the safe: birth date; car reg; telephone number. None of them worked. Harmony rifled through drawers in his bedroom and found Jeremy's passport. They tried that number. It worked.

Inside was all they were looking for. The original ROSE-BUD file, with all of Mr Parker's information on a print-out. A sheet of paper full of Arthur Parker signatures, as if someone was trying to copy it. Also, a video cassette with a very interesting cover. Harmony put it in her pocket. Then the front door opened and Jeremy came in. Harmony hid behind a door and Gregory just managed to dive into the kitchen. Luckily Jeremy went straight to the bathroom and started running a shower. Gregory went to the front door and opened it. Harmony was about to join him when she saw a movement under the bed. It was Monty and he was nibbling some airline tickets. Harmony went over and grabbed Monty and the tickets and crept along the hall.

Minutes later they were on the street. They'd done it! The next morning Mrs Parker was arranging for her husband's appeal.

CHAPTER 14

The courtroom was packed. Mr Parker sat in the dock, looking pale and ill. Harmony sat with Mrs Parker, Gregory and Grandma. Melody sat on the other side of the room with Jeremy. Mrs Parker told the judge that she was going to conduct the case herself. She questioned Gregory, then Harmony, then Jeremy Trelawn was called to give evidence.

Mrs Parker showed him the page of signatures. He denied the handwriting was his. She showed him the slightly nibbled airline tickets. They were to Brazil and in the names of Jeremy Trelawn and Helen Brodin, who worked with him. Melody looked taken aback but stayed sitting where she was. Jeremy said it was merely a business trip.

'In that case, why are the tickets one way?' Mrs Parker asked.

Jeremy faltered and said it was a mistake.

'How could you?' Melody asked, starting to feel foolish.

'Melody! Calm down,' Jeremy said.

'But we're meant to be getting married!'

'No we're not!' Jeremy turned to the judge. 'I'm afraid this girl just assumed . . .'

'Assumed nothing! You wrote me this letter,' and Melody took out the letter and read it aloud to the court:

'"I fell in love with you at first sight. Age doesn't matter, so please, please, say you'll marry me. Your ardent admirer, Kiss kiss kiss."'

'I didn't write that!' Jeremy said.

'You did!' Melody said.

'No he didn't. I did!' said the elderly clerk.

There was a stunned silence.

'*You* wrote it?!' the judge asked his clerk.

'Yes. To this dear lady,' the clerk said, pointing to Grandma.

Melody was in tears. She went to join Harmony and Grandma. Harmony even held her sister's hand.

Despite the evidence, Jeremy pointed out that he had admitted nothing criminal and that all the so-called 'evidence' had been obtained by breaking into his flat. The judge agreed and was about to close the case yet again and have Mr Parker sent back to prison, when Harmony stood and approached the jury.

'Grogsy and I did break into the flat, but we had to. Because my dad's been framed. By Jeremy Trelawn. With the court's permission I'd like to call Sir Anthony Snouch.'

And Sir Anthony was called. Except that, as Harmony showed, he wasn't Sir Anthony Snouch, but Joe Capon, an actor who specialized in courtroom dramas. Harmony had the video evidence to prove it, which she had found in Jeremy's safe. The judge was furious that he'd been fooled into thinking this oaf was a great lawyer.

That did it. Half an hour later Mr Parker was a free man.

Harmony thought that if the wishes left with the Queen's Nose could be hers alone, then she would wish to have Anita the rabbit and Lucky the dog back. Whether it was the coin or not, they were there at the flat when the Parkers got home.

Mr Parker was awarded compensation, but he had no desire for his old job. He wanted to open a garden centre, which is exactly what he and Mrs Parker later did. Grandma decided that the clerk was someone worth marrying, especially as he could play poker. Gregory and Melody became friends, which was probably the best thing. Anything else was too complicated.

Jeremy went to prison.

A few evenings later Harmony was on the roof garden. She turned and there was Uncle Ginger. He smiled and they hugged. Then she did what she knew he wanted her to – she took the Queen's Nose and threw it high in the air. It was time to let it go.